SOMEWHERE, HOME

Nada Awar Jarrar was born and brought up in the Lebanon by an Australian mother and a Lebanese father. She has subsequently lived in Australia, France, the US and the UK. She moved to the Lebanon seven years ago and lives in Beirut with her husband, Bassem. *Somewhere, Home* is her first work of fiction.

Nada Awar Jarrar

SOMEWHERE, HOME

V

VINTAGE

Published by Vintage 2004

2 4 6 8 10 9 7 5 3 1

First published in Great Britain in 2003 by
William Heinemann

Vintage
Random House, 20 Vauxhall Bridge Road,
London SW1V 2SA

Random House Australia (Pty) Limited
20 Alfred Street, Milsons Point, Sydney
New South Wales 2061, Australia

Random House New Zealand Limited
18 Poland Road, Glenfield,
Auckland 10, New Zealand

Random House (Pty) Limited
Endulini, 5A Jubilee Road, Parktown 2193,
South Africa

The Random House Group Limited Reg. No. 954009
www.randomhouse.co.uk

A CIP catalogue record for this book
is available from the British Library

ISBN 0 09 944317 1

Papers used by Random House are natural, recyclable products made from wood grown in sustainable forests. The manufacturing processes conform to the environmental regulations of the country of origin

Printed and bound in Great Britain by
Cox & Wyman Limited, Reading, Berkshire

For my family

PART I

MAYSA
Winter

This house, my house, saw its beginnings with the marriage of my grandfather. Built to hold the family in its overflowing numbers, the house became a meeting place for grandparents, aunts, uncles, children and numerous cousins from surrounding villages, its rooms expanding around them like sunlight in winter.

My father, Adel, remembers its high ceilings, the echo of footsteps on bare tiles and glimpses of his mother's long white veil floating through doorways behind her. At three, he once sat on the outside ledge of one of its arched windows and gestured towards the fields beyond, his own private kingdom, before falling into a prickly bush below and getting up a more humble boy. I remember, as a child, holding my hand against the hollow in my father's scalp and imagining I could feel the memory of that fall between my fingertips.

He would call me to him, 'Maysa, Maysa', and speak to me of his life in this house in fragments, in snatches of colour and longing, pausing to be the distant and more familiar figure of my childhood. But he did not know that it was his silences that intrigued me most, those moments between words that allow the imagination to wander.

I saw the brown dust of unpaved roads wrapping themselves round the mountain like arms entwined. I saw

the sun on those roads and the air that carried it. I saw
stone houses and armies of men and women in black and
white sitting in front of them, their hands spread fanlike
on their knees, their eyes squinting in the sun. I saw my
grandparents, Alia and Ameen, and their five children
sitting on low seats round a wood-burning stove in
winter, their cheeks flushed red, their hands reaching
towards the warmth, their voices low and intimate.

Now, years after they have all gone, as Beirut smolders
in a war against itself, I have returned to the mountain to
collect memories of the lives that wandered through this
house as though my own depended on it. And as my heart
turns further inward, I nurture a secret wish that in telling
the stories of those who loved me I am creating my own.
The village hangs against the side of a mountain. The
mountain grows pine trees and wild thyme, and is no
longer home to wild boar and wolf dogs. My grandmother told us, as children, of the famine that struck
during the Great War and the fear felt by men walking
through the night with sacks of Damascene wheat on their
backs, watching for animals that might attack.

The mountain seems tame now by comparison. I stand
at the front door and stare lazily into the garden. It is
almost autumn, almost cold, almost the end of freedom
and summer. At five o'clock the mist appears and hangs
listlessly over the house, over its crumbling red-brick roof
and around its jagged stone walls. It floats over fig trees
and grapevines, and ripens waiting fruit until it is ready for
picking. I touch the vine that hangs from the roof and

winds its way through the pointed arches that frame the front of the house. It runs along the rusty green balustrade at one end of the terrace overlooking an empty field and the village beyond, and edges towards the faltering wooden front door.

Since my arrival several weeks ago, I have been busily preparing for the cold winters that invade the mountain. Most of my things are now in the large room adjoining the kitchen. My bed is tucked into one corner with a large sofa across from it, and in between them is a Persian carpet woven in red geometric patterns that once belonged to my mother, Leila. Lined up against one of the walls is my grandmother's oak dressing table which has a full-length mirror stained with age and a secret drawer that no longer opens.

In the centre of the room I have installed the old wood-burning stove where I will boil water for bathing and do most of my cooking throughout the winter months. The kindling wood and dry pine cones are in a large tin container next to the stove and the blocks of firewood that I bought last week are piled high behind the door. The kitchen cupboard is stored with jars of pickled cheeses and green olives, and cloth sacks filled with cracked wheat, lentils, beans and pine nuts line its shelves.

The weather gets colder. I spend much of my days wrapped in blankets sitting on the sofa with a large notebook and sharpened pencils in my hand. When the stove heats up, I breathe in the green scent of burning pine until my head swims with it. Then the notebook slides to the floor, the palm of my hand opens to release the pencils and the words escape and float up to the high ceiling.

In the early evenings I watch the short-lived sunsets, not with a dreaminess, but in a slow and deliberate way, until the sun becomes a part of me too, going down in a blaze of red. Everything beckons me then, the pine trees, the stars and the singing crickets.

At night, when the village falls silent, I sit in my room and listen to the now familiar creaks and sighs of this house and revel within its reluctant embrace. If sleep does not come easily, I lie in my bed and try to imagine old age and loneliness enveloping me, getting closer and closer until they touch my skin and there is no running away from them.

Selma, the midwife, has become a regular visitor. A tall, dark amazon in whom wisdom sometimes outweighs kindness, Selma is a second cousin once removed and chooses to remain in the village because 'the world out there is no better'. She cares for me as she would an errant younger sister who does not really deserve her sympathy. She does not ask me about Wadih, the father of my child, nor why I decided to return to the mountain after a lifetime in the city. During her morning visits we drink tea made from dried flowers and herbs, and nibble flat, hard biscuits flavored with cardamom and musk. Because I am thirty-two, Selma wants me to be examined by a doctor, but I tell her that my confidence in her abilities is so great that I am certain nothing will go wrong on the day.

After six years of marriage Wadih and I had both given up hope of having a child when I discovered I was pregnant four months ago. For several weeks I lived through something close to stupor, unsure whether to be happy or shocked and sensing in my husband an equal uncertainty. As we slept, exhausted with thinking, his body stretched itself so that it seemed somehow to pass over me, his breath like slow mist in the evening. I stared at him and pressed my hand to his brow, and wished he would wake up and catch me watching him.

'This city is no place to bring a child into,' I told my husband.

'What do you mean?' There was indignation in his voice. 'This is our home, Maysa.'

'What about the fighting? What if something happens to the baby because of this wretched war?'

'Our baby will be as safe as every other child in Beirut.'

I thought then how lonely a man seems when he is alone, the hesitation in his step, his brows pushed up in astonishment at the finality of solitude, his heart ready to embrace the first curious look, the first hand touching, willing to touch.

Whenever Wadih had something of beauty to show me, the sea rushing and indifferent, the magnificence of mountains in winter or the distance in a blue sky, he would place a hand on the back of my neck and absently rub the skin there until I felt whatever I was looking at move up my spine, down my arms and into my fingertips.

The day before I left for the village we went for a walk on the beach.

'It's not just about the fighting, is it?' he asked me.

'That house is where everything began, Wadih,' I whispered.

'And what about me, Maysa? What about me?'

He walked past me then, another lone figure in the sun, vulnerable and fiercely strong both, as we all are.

My world feels so small now, the house, the garden and the shadows in between. On the rare occasions when I go down to the village, I encounter no one who can lift my spirits. When she comes to see me, Selma tells me people have begun to talk. Your belly, she says, is going to be difficult to hide soon.

I tell her that I am not afraid of village talk.

'And the child,' she retorts. 'What about the child? What about its father?'

I stand in front of the dressing table and stare at my figure in the full-length mirror. My dark hair looks long and unkempt, and my face is forlorn. I place my hand on my belly and rub gently. I am nothing like my former self, less poised and more vulnerable.

To comfort myself I think that my child will be different from the rest. She will have my dark hair, the sultry green eyes of her father and her skin will glow somewhere between gold and olive. I shall call her Yasmeena and dress her in shades of blue and yellow, and she will grow up to recognize the scents of pine and gorse just like her mother.

It is winter and I am resigned to my fate. My concern for the wilting vine will not be silenced. I fetch the ladder and climb up high enough to touch the trellis and the rope-like, dry branches that have become of the once luxuriant plant. Looking up through the netting at the distant sun, I am overcome by dizziness and fall off the ladder. I lie on the ground for a moment or two, breathing in the mixed smell of earth and dust, and feeling a tingling through my body.

Selma arrives but she is less than sympathetic.

'I found blood.'

'Lie down and let me look at you,' she says, gently pushing me onto the bed. 'What made you do it?'

'The vine is dying.'

'Dying? It's coming on to winter. Of course it's dying. It'll come back to life next year.'

I turn my head to the wall, fight back tears and hope she does not notice my distress.

'Yes,' she says abruptly after completing the examination and walks into the bathroom to wash her hands.

'Yes, what?' I call to her with alarm.

'The baby may have been affected by the fall. We'll have to call in a doctor.' She comes back into the room.

'You know I don't want a doctor, Selma. You know that's why I have you.'

'I know that you care about this baby more than about your pride.'

This house, this old, dilapidated house, was once a castle, alive and spilling over with energy. My grandmother sat in a wooden-backed chair at the southern window, watching for the last of her children running home from school, and now there are shadows where she has been, shadows without sunlight, clouding my vision, filling me with fear.

The doctor is a small man with a smooth face and delicate features. We do not talk during the examination.

When he is done, he sits down on the edge of the chair opposite my bed, his brown doctor's bag placed by his feet. His voice is soft. 'Yes, well, the baby is all right, but you'll have to make sure this doesn't happen again.'

Outside, the morning is well under way. I can hear the revving of engines and the children who use my front garden as a short cut on their way to school. The smell of pine cones burning in the stove fills the room with a soft scent and I cannot stand this man's clinical distance. 'You think I should be having this baby in a hospital, don't you, doctor?'

He looks taken aback. Then he stands up and prepares to leave, holding a piece of paper in one hand and his bag in the other. 'I'll ask Selma to fill in this prescription for you. If you notice any more bleeding, please call me.'

Selma sees him to the door and returns to my bedside. 'I'll go and get that medicine for you now.' She pulls the bed sheets up so that they almost touch my chin. 'Do you need anything else?'

The defiance rushes from me and leaves a sudden fluttering fear behind it. I reach for my friend's arm. 'Why can't I be more like Alia?'

Selma's reply is gentle. 'Do you think Alia never had moments when she felt unsure of herself?'

'I don't know what to think any more,' I say with a sigh. 'I'm trying so hard to understand.'

'What is there to understand? Your grandmother was capable and dutiful like most women had to be at that time.' Selma pats me on the shoulder and stands up. 'You have no way of knowing all these things now, Maysa,' she says in a matter-of-fact voice.

'But I can imagine, can't I?' I call out as she walks out of the door.

My woman's body carries itself from this doorstep along the dirt road beyond and falters by the apple tree where children played it seems a hundred years ago. Like the yolk of an egg, I am alone and sheltered. I shift around on stiffening hips and wish for summer. I know that this journey I take, I take without guidance, without searching, without hope. I walk alone and into the sun.

I am wakeful again and feel regret inching its way into my resolve. I get up to feed the wood stove and place a concoction of flowers and herbs into a pot to make a hot drink.

Outside, there is unqualified silence. I begin to wonder if I would not manage to rest easier if I moved into another room. I wrap a thick blanket round myself, light a candle and tiptoe to the other side of the house where the four boys, my father and his brothers, once slept.

The room is spacious and bitterly cold. I can see them, Salam, Rasheed, Fouad and Adel, lying one against the other for warmth on mattresses placed together to accommodate their growing bodies. I hear their breathing and see the shadowy figure that makes her way into the room, and feel the gentle kisses she gives them on flushed cheeks.

'Boys may grow soft if shown too much affection,' my grandmother whispers. 'My boys will be men.'

I sigh and wrap the blanket more closely round my shoulders. I want to have worn a different history, begun a different past. I want to have been a Chinese warrior, a rounded Eskimo, or perhaps a Scottish prince. I want to have looked up at wider skies, walked through thicker forests, waited for longer winters. Anything but this weighted, haunted longing for a distant past.

I move to the large cupboard at one end of the room and pull at its rickety doors. I have been planning to clear it out for weeks. When I get it open, a cloud of dust rushes into the room and I step back for a moment. The cupboard is empty except for a pile of books on its bottom shelf. There are story books and school books, Arabic, History and Mathematics, each with a child's name inscribed on the inside front cover. I open a literature textbook that once belonged to my uncle Rasheed and imagine his small head bent over in reading, a pencil in his hand and his heart somewhere hopeful.

I lift my head and savour the infinite silence of the night. Memories and imaginings mix together in my mind so that I can no longer tell which is which. My breath becomes uneven. I return the textbook to the cupboard and just as I prepare to get up notice a thick, leather-lined notebook on top of the pile. I pick it up and blow some of the dust off its cover. When I open it, I realize that it is some kind of ledger, its yellowed pages lined with black and bold red ink. I leaf through it and in my excitement tear off one of the pages. The notebook is empty, no words to comfort or inspire me.

I crumple the torn paper in my hand, make a ball with it and throw it up in the air. I begin to tear out other pages from the notebook and scatter them around the room, then stop. I get up and return to my room, hugging the notebook to my chest. Its smell intrigues me, stale, musty, with a hint of the sharp scent of virgin paper. I sit on my bed, look at it in the weak light of the candle on the table beside me and reach for a pencil. I open the front cover of the notebook and turn to the first page where I write Alia's name in big letters across the top.

I once asked my grandmother if when they were very young she had ever wondered what her children's future would be. It was only months before Alia's death and she was very frail, escaping into a vast silence when she could, waiting patiently on her invalid's bed. I looked into her eyes, her skin was white and transparent, and her face, under the thin white veil that she still insisted on wearing, looked small and clean.

She placed her hand on my arm and pulled herself up slightly. 'I knew,' Alia said.

'You knew what they dreamed they would be?' I asked.

She shook her head with impatience and gripped my arm. Then she suddenly let go and laid her head back on the pillow. 'They were my dreams too,' she said before turning her head to the wall.

Late into the night, I lie down on the bed and close my eyes, the notebook resting loosely in my arms.

ALIA

Alia mistook her dissatisfaction for sorrow. Taking a moment's breath from children and home, she would stand at her doorstep and imagine she saw a tall ghost of a man walking towards her, striding as though he led the people behind him. Although he would vanish before she could make out his features, Alia guessed it was her husband, Ameen, forever in Africa, missing her, finally coming home. Wearing a long black skirt and top, her head covered in a diaphanous white veil that fell across her shoulders and down her back, Alia would see herself running towards the figure like a gull to the sea, wrapping him in wings and comfort.

Yet, on Ameen's infrequent visits home, with the children's excitement and the stir of his presence in the village, he seemed no more real than that figure she always imagined, so transparent was his touch, so short their time together. Between his coming and going, another baby would be made and she, left like Mother Nature, would have to fend for herself. Then her heart would sit inside her with nothing to lighten its dull, insistent thud.

On Alia's wedding day, crowds of men stood in the front yard of her new home, surrounding her husband Ameen, shaking his hand and wishing on him a dozen sons. Alia sat on a pedestal in the living room, the women around her in a neat semicircle, their voices echoing through the still new house like future memories.

At nineteen, Alia had been ready for marriage, ready to discard a transitory adolescence that had left her no wiser to the mysteries of adulthood. Ameen was her mother's choice, a second cousin whose enthusiasm for life and strength of will would lead to greater things. There was no courtship, little need for negotiation between the two families and, when the wedding day dawned on a bright summer morning, Alia felt her spirit soar at the possibilities before her.

They would continue to live in the small mountain village their families had inhabited for hundreds of years, a quiet haven balanced on the side of Mount Lebanon and named after the refuge of ancient gods.

Their new home, a one-story stone cottage near the village center, was Alia's comfort. She marvelled at its spaciousness and delighted in the opportunity to make her mark on its rooms, to fill its corners with the little knick-knacks she could not keep as a child. She placed seashells and colored stones on window ledges, and embroidered tiny flowers wherever she could: on bed linen and tablecloths, and even on the small cloth sack she used for making yogurt cheese. She especially loved her bedroom, revelling in the smooth texture of freshly laundered sheets and fluffy down pillows.

During the early morning chores that she carried out under the watchful eye of her mother-in-law, Alia would often linger at her bedroom door and contemplate the rays of sun that shimmered on the newly painted walls, then sigh with a secret delight. But she did not reckon on the weight of sudden responsibility. Left to her own devices for the first few months following her marriage, Alia woke one morning to her husband's expectations and felt herself turn into the diligent and obedient wife she was bound to be. The children arrived in quick succession.

The first son, Salam, the peaceful one, was born after two agonizing days of labor. The women in the family spent the weeks following his birth serving generous portions of sweet brown pudding garnished with pine nuts and almonds to all who came to congratulate them. Alia was glad it was a boy, praise was more easily received than the commiseration that would have followed the birth of a baby girl.

When Salam was two years old, Ameen told her he would leave for Africa to join a distant cousin who had made there a fortune in trade. Alia kept the fear that gripped her heart following Ameen's unexpected decision to herself, spending the last few nights before his departure in sleepless worry. Moments before leaving for the city to catch the boat for Africa, Ameen held her briefly to him and murmured a quiet goodbye. Though she did not know it, that was to be the most tender moment of her married life.

Salam grew into instinctive gentleness, loving his mother as he did the sea he had not seen, not understanding his father's long absences.

'He has gone to Africa to make our fortune,' his mother told him. 'Across the sea. Across the sea.'

The Mediterranean became for Salam a blueness that swallowed men and spat them out onto distant, hostile shores.

Three brothers came after him, Rasheed, Fouad and Adel. Alia saw in each of her sons the potential for destinies beyond the confines of the village they so loved. She groomed the three younger boys for future careers in law, medicine and engineering, and left them to revel in childhood. Salam, she knew, would follow his father as all first-born sons did. In the absence of Ameen, Alia was afraid to show the boys too much affection. She wanted them to grow strong, disciplined like their father, and would reproach them for weeping. She was convinced the emotional distance was more painful for her than for the children and did not waver from her resolve in their wakeful hours. But on long, quiet nights when her loneliness seemed too much to bear, Alia would steal into the boys' bedroom and, standing in the hollow of the open doorway, would watch the four of them as they slept.

Whenever their father came to visit, the children were wary of him until he shed his air of strange lands and smelled like them of the mountain. They would sit around him in the winter room, warming yogurt sandwiches on the stove, waiting for him to speak, to ask for something that they might obey. Wrapped in a greatcoat made from the finest camel hair, he looked as magnificent as an Arab prince, his skin darkened by another sun.

Though he never spoke of Africa, they knew he was as great a man there as he was in the village.

My father this, my father that, Salam boasted to other children, until he turned eighteen and went to work alongside his father in jungle dampness. There he saw the making of men's fortunes, travelling to and from tribal settlements and selling what he could of his goods, an apprentice in trade. As the years passed and his work expanded, Salam would take the time to sit on the porch of his wooden house enjoying the coolness of the evening, gazing at the stars that visited the skies of Africa and were so unlike those at home, dreaming of his return and leaving the dream to rest in a quiet corner of his heart.

Alia thought Rasheed the most beautiful of her children, with his evenly spaced eyes beneath gently arching eyebrows, his straight nose and small mouth that smiled in a graceful upward motion as if in quiet amusement. His demeanour suggested an aged serenity that, in a child, inspired awe in some, disbelief in others. In conversations with his mother, Rasheed would sometimes stop in mid-sentence and appear to give himself an almost imperceptible shake before suddenly picking up where he had left off. Alia began to fear that while blessed with the looks and manners of a patrician, Rasheed did not have the wisdom to cope with life, until the day he came to her as she sat on the edge of the bed, a letter from Ameen crumpled in the palm of her hand, the pain of disappointment clutching at her heart.

'He's not coming this year, is he?' asked Rasheed.

Alia shook her head.

'Your uncle Suleiman just read this to me,' Alia said, holding the letter up in her hand. 'No, he's not coming.'

Approaching his mother very slowly, the boy reached out and placed one small hand gently on her cheek, keeping it there until the tears trickled down onto his fingers. Rasheed treated all his brothers with equal gentleness, showing Fouad the special attention that as a middle child he was never able to solicit from the women in his young life.

Fouad was convinced his grandmother hated him and mistook his mother's confusion for rejection. 'I'll find him, I'll find him.' The four-year-old Fouad rubbed his eyes with small hands and lamented to himself.

'Where are you going, Fouad? Come here. Why are you crying?'

Sheikh Abu Khalil watched the child from astride his donkey.

'I'll find him,' muttered the little boy. 'I'll walk to Africa.'

'Africa. You want to go see your father? Come up and ride. I'll take you to Africa.'

Abu Khalil jumped off the donkey and lifted the boy onto the cloth saddle. They travelled back home in silence, Fouad finally asking, 'Is it much further? Is it much further to Africa?'

When, years later, Fouad was able to prove his brilliance by entering medical school at the age of sixteen, his father bought him a new pair of patent leather shoes that squeaked as he walked so that everyone could hear him coming.

At six years old Adel was a dark and thin boy with a quick temper and the long, fine fingers and toes of his father. Alia loved his nervous energy and agile mind, and would sometimes laugh quietly to herself if he got into trouble. As an infant, his grandmother favoured him above the rest, sang to him in her old woman's voice. He would look into her dried, sunken eyes as she rocked him and together they would remember past lives, dismissed by everyone but the very young and the ageless.

When he was three years old, Adel stepped outside one cold winter's morning and fell into several feet of snow that had accumulated in the front garden the night before. After an unsuccessful struggle to pull himself up, Adel sank further into the cocoon of snow and fell asleep. A tuft of thick dark hair was all that showed above the snow's surface. It was a while before Adel was finally found, almost frozen through, his small body curled into a stiff ball, his lips a frightening, ugly blue. Alia carried him inside, undressed him and wrapped him with her own body. Hours later, he pushed her arms away, looked slowly around him and fell into a long, sound sleep.

The children were at once vital and incidental to Alia's life. She would stop and watch them as they played, four bright-faced boys who loved her with an intensity that sometimes sent her own heart reeling so suddenly that she would wish herself far away and free of them. She could never bring herself to tell anyone about her fear of waking up one day and abandoning her children, choosing instead not to allow herself to love them too much.

As they began to grow older, Alia's hold over her sons did not diminish. Rather, they seemed to look to their mother for inspiration with even greater enthusiasm, the admiration of followers in their eyes. Between them, Salam, Rasheed, Fouad and Adel drew their mother's fate as surely as a timely premonition, setting their ambitions against her own and waiting for the future to unfold.

The day that Alia dreamed of changing her life began like any other. She helped the boys prepare themselves for school, made the thickly spread labneh sandwiches they would have for lunch and handed them each a stick of firewood for the classroom stove. Standing on the doorstep, she watched as Salam and Rasheed walked away with the two little ones in tow, a slowness in their step as they tried to shake the last remnants of sleep into wakefulness.

Just as Alia was about to walk back into the house, Rasheed stopped in his tracks and turned round to look straight at her. The early morning sun and gentle mist framed his tall, slim figure and his face in the distance seemed to give out a bright light. Alia's heart left her for one endless moment and skipped its way to her son, luminescent, reaching for home. Then Rasheed became a schoolboy again and turned away, his back slightly bent with reluctant defeat. He would, she knew, accompany his younger brothers to the village school and then, with Salam, trek several miles to his own in a nearby village.

When she heard of the accident, Alia was in the courtyard with her mother-in-law stirring a huge cauldron of tomato sauce which, once cooled, would be preserved in glass jars for winter stores. Alia's cousin Iman was running towards the house, her veil flailing behind her, her eyes wild.

'Alia, Alia,' Iman shouted. 'The boys. Hurry.'

Alia did not wait for Iman to reach her. She stood up, grabbed her skirt and flew towards her cousin.

'The school in Salima . . . Alia, it collapsed over the children and Salam and Rasheed are inside with the others.'

Alia stood still as a rush of fear made its way through her, sending a tingling feeling into her fingertips and down to her toes. She began to run. She ran down through the village souq, past the local school where her two younger boys were safe and sound. She ran the twisting, winding road that led to Salima as fast as the lithe hyena she had once glimpsed as a child on a walk in the woods. She ran, her long pigtail coming loose and trailing behind her, lightning beneath her feet. She shouted an angry pledge to God that if her boys survived the disaster she would never let longing into her heart again.

When she got to the school, she saw a group of men standing among the rubble shouting instructions to one another and attempting to lift the large pieces of limestone that had been the single-storey school building. Dozens of bewildered-looking young boys covered with dust wandered around the school grounds, some weeping, others silent. Alia's eyes skimmed over their faces, her heart thumping.

'Mama, Mama.'

She felt two pairs of thin young arms wrap themselves round her and looked down to see her sons looking up at her. She held them tightly to her and kissed the tops of their heads, and felt unable to speak.

On the way back home Alia learned that Salam had jumped onto a window ledge as soon as the rumbling began.

'But Rasheed was at the lunch table with the others, Mama,' Salam said. 'He was the only one to survive.'

Alia grasped Rasheed's hand a little tighter and repeated a silent prayer.

Later that night, as the children slept, Alia tiptoed out of the house and made her way to the small church that stood at the heart of the Christian area of the village. Hesitating, she pushed the large wooden door open and went in. She had never believed she would one day see the inside of a church and was taken aback by the thick, calm air that filled the near-darkness.

A priest with a large cloth in his hand was wiping objects on a big, rectangular table at one end of the room. He looked up as Alia approached. 'Yes?' he asked, until she came up close. 'Welcome, welcome. You're Ameen's wife, aren't you?'

Alia hung her head.

'Is everything all right?' the priest continued. 'Shall we go outside and sit down?'

She nodded and followed the priest into the courtyard.

'How can I help you, my daughter?' he asked her once they had sat down.

'I need you to write a letter for me. It's very important.'

He nodded and waited for her to continue.

'It's to my husband. He's in Africa and I need him to come home. I . . .' Alia squeezed her eyes shut and hoped the priest hadn't seen in them the beginning of tears.

'I'll help you write the letter,' he said. 'Don't worry, my dear. No one will know about this but the two of us.'

Alia sighed with relief and lifted her head to the sky.

My husband Ameen,

God willing you are well and happy in distant Africa. We are all fine here, thank God, and everyone asks after you. The priest is writing this letter for me and I am grateful to him for that because these words belong only to you now.

When the sun begins to set and the boys are washed and fed and preparing to sit quietly over their school work, there is whispering in our house, a relief in our voices at the blessed ending of another day, a kind of resignation too. That is when I think of you most, of the scent of you and the way your arms swing briskly at your sides when you walk. And as I close my eyes and let the hush sweep over me, I imagine your body brushing noiselessly past my own and begin to dream of a more certain touch.

And try as I might, Ameen, even deep in the night when I am in bed and restless, I cannot see your face; your features, fine and grave, escape me. Are his eyes round or almond-shaped? I ask myself. Does his brow crease when he thinks and do his lips droop or disappear in anger?

Then other questions come to mind about what your life is like so far away and whether you have found your own comforts there, your own release. I pray for you.

Salam is grown and will soon be ready to join you in Africa. Rasheed, Fouad and Adel wait for you as I do. God be with you.

Your wife
Alia.

It was that secret hour between dawn and waking, and Alia stood leaning against the doorway of her home, gazing at the village below. Behind her the sleeping sounds of four boys and their father floated in and out of the spacious rooms, muffled in dreams. She lifted her hands and laid them against her cheeks, then took a deep breath of the sharp spring air and stepped slowly out into the courtyard.

The village was quiet. Rows of umbrella pines stood still and tall, dotted among the stone houses and the narrow dirt road that wound its way between them. In the distance she could make out the moving figures of Milad, the milk-seller, and his donkey. For one moment she imagined she heard the clanking sound of the tin cans filled with pungent goat's yogurt as they bumped against one another on top of his saddle. In the pink sky overhead, thin clouds of smoke wafted out of a lone chimney and vanished into the morning.

Someone besides myself is awake then, Alia said to herself.

She placed her hand on her lower belly and tried to feel for the budding child she knew was there. This time it would be a girl and she would name her Saeeda.

Alia shook her head and reached down to pluck at a weed wedged between the cobblestones at her feet. The courtyard was strewn with dry pine needles and needed a thorough sweeping. When she straightened up and turned towards the house, catching sight of the four pointed arches outlining the porch and the red-brick rooftop slanted evenly above them, she felt a sudden rush of pleasure. 'Our house,' she whispered. 'Our beautiful house.'

MAYSA
Spring

The vine is coming back to life. I can see bright green shoots pushing out of its branches that revel in the sun and make tiny shadows on the tiled floor below. Every morning I carry a plateful of fruit and a cup of flower tea out to the terrace, sit on an old sofa I have placed there and stare out at the view. The village wakes with a start, to the sound of children preparing for school and shop-keepers rolling up the corrugated-iron fronts of their shops, to the smell of wood stoves being relit and the sight of the thin white smoke that rises from them.

Soon after the first small commuter bus inches its way up a steep hill and away to the city, cars appear, dozens of them that whiz up and down the main road. By then, the movement of people and machines appears almost frenetic and I carry the remains of my breakfast back into the quiet of my house lest the anxiety invade me too. There, I wonder how different Alia's mornings must have been, the duties of house and children to see to, stretching her days into a fever of physical activity. She once told me that she had always favoured early mornings in the village, those moments before the children woke up, when the house pulsed with their collective heartbeat and she could stop and contemplate her fortune.

I look down at my now huge belly that hangs low and

round over my legs and feet. I wear different versions of large, comfortable sweatsuits that have only just begun to strain against my widening girth. Selma has cut my hair so that it frames my face in a curly dark cap and lifts the circles from under my eyes. My skin has lost its flaky winter appearance and glows with the freshness of the mountain air. If I did not know better, I would believe Selma when she tells me that a woman who grows prettier as her pregnancy advances is carrying a girl.

The doctor, I know, already has an inkling of the gender of my child, but after the tests I have taken at his clinic he has refrained from telling me which it is and I have feigned indifference. He has extracted from me a promise that I will let him know as soon as labour pains begin and that I will be willing to go to a nearby hospital if he thinks it necessary. 'We have to think of the baby.'

Alia had all her babies at home, with her mother-in-law and a local midwife in attendance. It was a matter of life or death every time but she always got through it. What it must have felt like to greet each of those babies, their sudden plop into being, a startled screech and the touch of roughened mother-hands on slippery, transparent skin. Did she cherish the approval of the family and indulge in the brief admiration shown her by her husband when he was there?

'What does it matter either way?' Selma says to me.

I shake my head and tell her I don't understand.

'What does it matter what anyone thinks or says,' she continues. 'All you can do is just get on with it.'

Maybe that's what Alia knew she had to do. I am surprised into silence at the thought. 'You mean she may not have thought about it at all?' I ask Selma.

'I mean she accepted her fate like most women did in those days.'

But I don't believe that, I begin to say and then stop. 'What was it, then? What did she really feel?' I ask instead.

The truth is that I don't know. I strain to remember the look in her eyes and come up with little more than a mixture of tenderness and distance, the look of a woman with secrets that she will not disclose to a child. Did she love Ameen or had he merely been a part of a destiny she could not avoid? Did she really long to go with him to Africa and did she miss him when he left? Who was her favorite of the children, who held that special place in her heart?

'If Alia hardened her resolve when it came to bringing up the boys, then what softness was left over for Saeeda?' I ask Selma. 'She married off her only daughter before Ameen knew anything about it.'

'She had no choice,' Selma retorts. 'Girls could not be left to fall in love on their own, especially if they were as flighty as Saeeda was.'

'You remember my aunt?'

'Yes, of course I do. You do as well, don't you?'

Saeeda had a small dark mole just above her top lip that moved as she spoke. I remember watching it with intense fascination when I was a child. My aunt took care of Alia and Ameen during the last years of their lives, and we saw her whenever we went up to the village for a visit. Until I moved back to the mountain, my interest in Saeeda had always been superficial.

'She never told those children that she loved them,' I say.

'She didn't need to,' Selma replies. 'They already knew it.'

'No. Children don't just know,' I protest.

I place my hands on my belly and rub gently at the stretching skin beneath my clothes.

'But they always find out when they grow up,' Selma says. 'That you love them, I mean.'

'Is that what you're hoping will happen with your own children, Selma?'

She is offended, mutters a quick goodbye and leaves the house.

Spring makes its way into my heart and lifts my spirit. I have the wood stove removed from my room and place the bed underneath the window that faces the front garden. Hovering between sleep and waking in the early morning, I breathe in long and deep and imagine living on the mountain for ever, my child and I self-contained in our splendid, crumbling house. I air out the rooms of the house, and watch the sunlight sweep over the rooftop and stream through the open windows.

Father, dreamer, your thoughts are still hanging in the air of this house, wandering and waiting for you. Do you remember the day you held our hands, my brother Kamal's and mine, and swung us into the air of this garden? Mother, the silence here is you, the graceful movement of your head turning away and your quiet, wistful step. I think of you both, your plunge into old age, a final acquiescence, a fitting goodbye.

I see Alia shuffling around in old age, dreaming of her boys, a businessman, a lawyer, a doctor and an engineer. They left her, married and had children of their own, taking the city for their permanent home and believing, as all men do, in their immortality. Until they stumbled into complicated lives that demanded the resourcefulness and expanse of vision they had learned from Alia and Ameen.

I wonder how much of their anxiety Alia really felt and have a wish that she showed each of them a moment's weakness, a taste of unclouded tenderness.

Selma loosens my worries over the impending birth as she would a stubborn knot, visiting me in the evenings and clattering about the house with practiced efficiency. She has put aside clean sheets, towels and two new pillows, and placed them in a plastic bag on top of the bedroom cupboard. 'We will need them all when the time comes,' she says with authority.

She tells me my single bed will be too small for the baby and me, and orders a new and larger mattress, which a handyman places over Alia's old bed in the adjoining room. Her fussing comforts me but makes me feel somehow apart from the coming event and the anxiety begins to return.

'All right, what is it now?' Selma asks with gruff tenderness.

I shake my head, watch as tears fall on the crisp white baby sheets on my lap.

Selma sits on the bed beside me. 'It's not unusual to be feeling like this so near your time.'

'Yes. You've told me before,' I whisper, suddenly realizing that just this once it is not Selma I want beside me.

She pats me lightly on the back and gets up again. 'It's time I left,' she says, making another of her unexplained departures.

I take the notebook from my bedside table and go out to the terrace. It is early afternoon and I have been unable to find comfort in sleep. I feel heavy and lethargic, and my feet are slightly swollen. I lower myself onto the sofa, rest my legs up on it and place a pillow behind my back. When I open the notebook, I am pleased at the sight of pages that are filled with words, at the names of those who came before and are here no longer, indelible now, but I still cannot explain the hollowness in my heart.

I turn to a new page and write Saeeda's name at the top.

SAEEDA

Saeeda was the last child, the happy one, a girl. She had rosy cheeks and dark hair, and as an infant showed an inclination for joy that none in her family possessed.

Alia's feelings for her daughter wavered between love and irritated concern until the day she promised five-year-old Saeeda's hand in marriage to a first cousin's son and no longer felt the need to worry about her future.

Asaad was only thirteen at the time and was already half in love with an olive-skinned and indolent village girl who lived on the other side of the village. Alia had watched one day while Asaad gazed in awe at the girl as she sauntered back from the village spring, a clay jar perched on one of her shoulders, her arms lifted to steady it so that her dress swung high above thin ankles and small feet. As she knelt to rest her jar on the roadside, a gold cross appeared round her neck and swung between the two small breasts bound by her bodice.

Saeeda never knew of her mother's plans for her, nor of the overwhelming sadness they would make of her life, and grew up thinking the world of herself. Her brothers loved her with guilt-ridden indulgence, trying to make up for the indifference she would encounter as a grown woman. Adel, who was closest to Saeeda in age, was fiercely protective of his sister, fighting off any attempts to harm her, assuring her that she was as good as any boy he knew.

But whenever he urged her to find the strength to hit back at trouble, she would shake her dark head and smile. 'You're my courage, Adel. There's enough anger in you for both of us.'

That was when he determined to look out for her for the rest of their lives.

Like her brothers, Saeeda attended the village school, but unlike them her enthusiasm was for the company rather than the learning. She was an unexceptional student who would incite her friends into spontaneous laughter and smile as soon as the teacher approached to reprimand them.

The only uncertainty Saeeda felt was in her mother's presence, sensing Alia's restless heart and wanting to reassure her. Saeeda would often rush in from the garden to sit by her mother and reach out to touch her hand lightly. Alia would look up from whatever she was doing and smile at the little girl, before turning away without seeing the light in her daughter's eyes falter.

In early adolescence Saeeda refused to wear the long white veil her mother had ordered for her from Damascus, tentatively touching the delicate white silk and then pulling her hand away.

'What is it, Saeeda?' Alia asked.

Saeeda shook her head and did not answer.

'Is it the material? It's the best silk to be found anywhere.'

Saeeda looked at her mother and replied in a whisper, 'I don't want to cover my hair.'

'What do you mean? You know very well that all the women in the family do.'

'I won't cover my hair!' Saeeda said before stomping out of Alia's room.

Later that day Saeeda found the veil neatly folded in a small square on her bed. She picked it up and gently shook it out. She scrunched the material in one hand and lifted it up to her cheek. It was softer than she had imagined and smelled faintly of the olive oil soap her mother used to wash her hands. Tiptoeing across the hall, Saeeda sneaked into Alia's bedroom and walked up to the dressing table. She placed the veil on her head and watched the folds of silk fall over her narrow shoulders. She lifted one end of the cloth, threw it over one side and admired the way the whiteness set off her black hair and rosy cheeks. I am beautiful, she thought, and twirled lightly round.

'Saeeda, what are you doing?' Adel stood in the doorway watching her.

Saeeda tore the veil off her head, and rushed out of the room and into the garden. Alia was tending to her flowers and did not see Saeeda run as fast as her legs would take her to the pine forest behind the village school. She buried the veil and returned home.

When Saeeda married at fifteen, her father and eldest brother were not there to see the despair in the young groom's eyes. He was dressed up, his hair combed back, and after the wedding was sent home with a child on his arm, a child unaware of the dramatic turn her life was about to take. The marriage lasted less than a year, cut short by the groom's sudden departure for South America. He was never heard of again.

Saeeda lost her little-girl look and took on the responsibility of caring for her departed husband's parents. Until their deaths the old couple took from her all the attention they thought their due. Unused to housework, Saeeda did her best to keep their home clean and tidy, looking for corners to wipe dust away from as she had seen her mother do, scrubbing the old people's clothes with the natural soaps she bought from the village souq and hanging them out to dry on the front-yard clothesline.

On early summer mornings Saeeda would reluctantly get out of bed and check on her in-laws, and coax them into the armchairs she had placed on the front terrace where they could watch the comings and goings of their neighbours. Then she would rush into the kitchen, boil some flower tea and make the labneh sandwiches they loved. As she sat talking to them, asking after their health, insisting on an enthusiasm for the day that she did not feel, her thoughts would wander to her childhood and the endless joy some moments had held.

She thought back to Thursday nights when her mother wore a long white veil of Damascene silk wrapped tightly round her head, covering her soft hair and showing only familiar eyes. 'I'm going to the prayer reading,' she would tell the children through silk. 'You may sit outside and listen. Quietly, children.' They would sit and stare at the rows of polished shoes arranged neatly outside the prayer room beside Grandfather's grave. It was there Saeeda committed the most magnificent act of defiance of her life. Sneaking past her waiting brothers, she grabbed an armful of shoes and threw them across the garden before reaching out for more. Then, cheeks flushed and eyes sparkling, she turned from her staring brothers, laughing loudly, her head flung back, and ran away. She was married a year later.

When her in-laws died, Saeeda returned home to live with Alia and Ameen, and at twenty-eight prepared once again to put the comfort of others before her own. She watched the two people who, one in her presence and the other in his absence, had shaped her life and loved them with the same intensity she had as a child, the anxiety she had once felt turning into insistent tenderness. She took over the running of the house, working quickly and quietly, her efforts imperceptible, mindful of her parents as she might have been of the children she never had.

Alia did not know what to do with the woman Saeeda had become. She would watch her daughter doing the housework and prepare to criticize a mattress unturned or a floor left unswept when something would stop her and the words refused to make themselves heard. In time, Alia realized that her heart had begun to dictate her actions. The tears that doctors told her were the result of the stroke she had suffered came to her without warning, trickling down to the taste of salt in her mouth. If Saeeda noticed her mother's sadness, she did not comment on it, discreetly handing the older woman a handkerchief and then moving on to something else.

Saeeda's attachment to her father grew as he became older and more vulnerable. Whenever he complained of pain in his arthritic hands, she would pour a spoonful of olive oil into her own and gently massage it into his long fingers, rubbing slowly at the swollen joints and humming a quiet tune to soothe him. Once, as she reached out to take his hand, he lifted it, placed it lightly on her face and smiled with such sweetness that Saeeda thought her heart would drop.

'Are you all right, Father?' she asked him.

'You're a good child,' he whispered in his old man's voice. 'A good child.'

When Ameen died, Saeeda had just turned forty-two. She was rounder than she had once been, but her black eyes still betrayed hope and the rosy white complexion that had always been her only claim to beauty had not withered. Her mother was by then feeble.

Saeeda's brothers insisted on bringing in a middle-aged widow from a nearby village to help care for Alia.

With extra time on her hands, Saeeda decided to tend to the long-neglected garden of the family home. She began by clearing it of the debris that had accumulated over the years, making way for the herb and flower beds she planned for, and raking the pebbles out of the earth. She scrubbed the floor of the terrace clean until the criss-cross pattern on the tiles that covered it shone in the sun, and had the iron balustrade around its edges painted with the same dark-green color as the front door. She planted a clinging vine that would climb up the balustrade and enclose the terrace in green. Then she placed tall yellow rose bushes at the end of the garden overlooking the souq, and pink and red geraniums just behind them where they could be seen from the terrace.

But it was the herb garden that Saeeda was most proud of, a small square plot just outside the kitchen door, which she filled with basil and thyme, parsley, mint, rosemary and coriander, everything she loved to touch and smell and taste in her cooking. She spent so much time tending this part of the garden that the heady scents seeped into her clothes and skin, and stayed there so that she only had to lift her hands to her face and the smell of fresh basil mixed with the sharpness of parsley, mint and the exotic aroma of thyme and coriander would fill her nostrils.

Villagers said that it was the fragrance emanating from that herb garden that lured the stranger to Saeeda's doorstep one summer afternoon. He carried a large sack of unshelled peanuts in one hand, a gray felt fedora in the other.

Saeeda and Alia had been sitting on the terrace in the imperfect shade of the still young vine, sipping aniseed tea in silence. Saeeda put down her cup and walked up to the man. He was small, thin and had the kind of face that from a distance seems familiar. She thought at first that he had lost his way, until he asked to see her father.

'My father passed away over a year ago,' Saeeda said, shaking her head.

'May the loss be compensated in your own life.' He paused before adding, 'I once worked with your father in Africa. I wanted so much to see him and thank him for all he did for me.'

Khaled came from a small village across the mountain. Returning home after a twenty-year absence, he carried the mystery of distant places about him that Saeeda's father once had. She sat Khaled next to her mother, served him tea and sweetmeats, and listened to the stories of adventure Ameen had neglected to tell her and her brothers. When he left some time later, the two women made their way into the house and prepared for bed.

'I never knew Father had such an exciting time of it in Africa,' Saeeda said.

Alia grunted.

Saeeda could feel her mother's eyes following her around the room. 'Is everything all right, Mother?' Saeeda turned and asked.

Alia only looked at her daughter more closely.

'Let's go to bed, then.'

Khaled came regularly after that, sometimes as often as three times a week, always carrying a gift for Saeeda and her mother, always with a smile on his small, angular face. Saeeda was welcoming though she did not quite understand his interest. He was nothing like her beloved brothers, all with families of their own, strong and no longer needing her or their mother. Khaled was fragile, a man whose energy seemed finally to have dissipated after years of exile and hard work. In Saeeda he seemed to find the pause from activity that he needed, the quietness of a resigned existence. They sometimes spoke for hours, Khaled telling her of his years in Africa, Saeeda recounting stories of her childhood. At others they would sit in silence, watching the movement of the village around them and fussing over Alia if she sat with them.

Saeeda began to look forward to Khaled's visits, not allowing her thoughts to wander beyond them but sensing suppressed anticipation inside her nonetheless.

One evening Khaled arrived later than usual to find Alia already in bed and Saeeda preparing to follow. 'I'm sorry,' he said, standing at the front door. 'I must be disturbing you.'

'Come in, Khaled.' Saeeda opened the door wider. 'Come in.' She showed him into the living room where a small side lamp cast shadows across the walls. 'Can I get you anything?' she asked him.

'No, no, please. I just want to talk to you.'

Saeeda sat down and looked closely at Khaled. Suddenly she felt uneasy.

'We are friends, you and I, aren't we?' he began.

She nodded.

'I feel I can tell you anything and you would understand.'

Saeeda smiled.

'They want me to get married!'

'They?'

'The family. There's a cousin from our village, they want me to marry her . . .' He got up and began pacing up and down the room.

Saeeda's heart raced and her eyes followed his every movement.

'They don't know,' Khaled continued. He turned and looked straight at her. 'I already have a family back there. I told you about it, didn't I?' he said. 'We never married. She is African.'

Saeeda shook her head in disbelief and continued to stare at Khaled.

'I left her and the children, thinking I would be able to stay away,' he said, sitting down next to her. 'Your father knew about it. He understood, was so kind.' He started to cry.

Saeeda reached for him and then pulled her hand away. She was surprised at how angry she was.

Khaled looked up at her and opened his eyes wide when he saw the look on her face. 'I thought you would understand, Saeeda.'

She folded her arms over her heart. 'We can't all be loved the way we want to be.'

His once fine face seemed suddenly ungenerous and pinched. She looked away.

'I'm sorry. I just came to let you know, I'm leaving the country next week. You won't see me again.'

The next day Saeeda was clearing up in the kitchen after lunch. When Alia got up from the table, Saeeda turned to her. 'Mother, what do you say we take the tea out on the terrace?'

The air was fresh and a subtle breeze lifted the green vine leaves into a gentle flutter. The two women settled themselves on the old sofa. Saeeda leaned over and poured the tea. She handed her mother a cup and took one for herself. It was that quiet hour between day and sunset, when village life seemed to float as if on an afterthought.

Saeeda felt a sudden impatience. 'Did you love my father?' she asked her mother.

Alia stared back at her. 'What do you mean?'

'Just that. Did you love your husband, Mother?'

'In those days no one talked about love,' Alia replied firmly. 'I saw little of Ameen through most of our marriage, until he turned old and needed me to care for him.'

Saeeda looked at her mother and felt a deep, wide anger moving through her body. She had a sudden urge to get up and run, anywhere, away from her mother's indifference, beyond the house and the village and everything she had ever known. 'Did you at least miss him?' she asked, trying to keep her voice even.

Alia put her cup down, bent her head and placed her hands in her lap. When she looked up, her face had the waxed look of age all over it. 'I wrote him a letter once, asking him to come home,' she said with a weak smile. 'It was after the two older boys were hurt when the school collapsed over them.' She shook her head and looked past Saeeda. 'I never sent it.'

Why didn't you let him know you needed him, Mother? Saeeda wanted to ask, until she remembered what had happened to her the night before and the enormity of her own fears.

'Does that man want to marry you?' Alia had recovered herself.

'You mean Khaled?'

'He was here last night, wasn't he?'

'Yes, he was.'

'What was he thinking, coming so late?'

'It wasn't that late, Mother. I had been planning on staying up a little longer anyway.'

'Does he want to marry you?' Alia persisted.

'No, Mother,' Saeeda said, shaking her head. 'I don't love him. I don't want to leave our home. I never have.'

MAYSA
Summer

I wake to the sound of someone knocking on the front door. The early mornings are still cool and I wrap myself in a blanket before going to open the door. Wadih is standing on the terrace with a small suitcase in one hand and a large leather folder in the other. He has no jacket on. 'Come in,' I tell him.

He walks past me and stands in the hallway for a moment.

'Come through here.' I point to my room. 'Just give me a moment to get dressed and make us some tea.'

He places his things on the floor and sits on the unmade bed.

'Will you wait?' I ask him.

He nods his head and looks away. This, I think to myself, is the moment I usually feel anger at his silences. I take my clothes into the bathroom and shut the door.

When I come out again, Wadih is not in the room. I run a hand through my wet hair and go into the kitchen to find him stirring a pot of flower tea, his head bent low over the fragrant steam floating from it.

'It smells wonderful, doesn't it? Like a garden in spring.'

'Wonderful.' Wadih is smiling.

'Let's have the tea out on the terrace,' I say, putting cups and saucers on a tray and grabbing the biscuit box.

We carry the things outside and make ourselves comfortable on the sofa, now warm with the early morning sun. Wadih pours the tea and hands me a cup. I place it on the table, put my hands on top of my belly, feeling for our child.

'It's very soon, isn't it?' he asks, looking down at my hands.

'I'm having it here in the house.'

'Yes, I thought you would.'

I feel a sudden remorse. 'There will be a doctor with the midwife in case of any problems,' I tell him. 'I've had all the tests and everything. It's going to be all right.'

'Did you find your stories?' Wadih asks after a short silence.

'Stories?'

'Your grandmother and her family, did you find out about her? You talked about it so much, I just assumed . . .'

I had forgotten telling him. It was long ago, very soon after we met. I said I wanted to spend time on my own on the mountain to gather stories about my grandmother and her children and put them in a book to read to my own children one day.

Wadih leans forward in his seat and looks closely at me. His eyes, the lines in his handsome face are achingly familiar and I feel the urge to reach out and touch him. Instead, I stand up and pick at branches of the vine that are draped over the balustrade.

'Are things all right in the city these days?' I ask my husband.

'The fighting flares up and calms down again. We manage to live during the gaps in between.'

'I haven't felt lonely,' I tell him.

'Nor have I,' he replies. 'I only missed you.'

I return to the sofa. 'I missed you too,' I say truthfully. 'I haven't really discovered anything new, but I've been trying to write my own thoughts down, my own unfocused musings.' I laugh sheepishly and look up at him but he says nothing.

A rush of heat makes its way up into my face and I place my hands on my cheeks in an attempt to cool them. 'That silence,' I say, 'that relentless, obstinate silence, it makes me feel unloved.'

Wadih gets up and goes into the house. He returns with the leather folder he brought with him, places it on the dusty tiles and unzips it open. Inside there is a small pile of white cardboard squares with drawings on them. He brings the top one to me. The drawing looks remarkably like my house except that the façade is much neater, the rooftop is even and the terrace is wider underneath the clean stone arches.

Wadih brings me the second drawing. This one is of the inside of the house. There is a bright kitchen that opens onto a large dining room, and the living room is spacious and colourful with furniture and patterned Persian carpets. 'This is of the bedrooms,' he says, handing me the third drawing. 'I think we'd have to add on another bathroom, especially now the baby is coming.'

I pull at his sleeve. 'What is this?'

'You do want us to live here, don't you? The house will have to be renovated so I made some preliminary drawings for you to look at before we make a final decision.'

'Did Selma tell you to come here?' I ask him.

He reaches out and places his hand on the back of my neck and rubs gently at my skin. 'Does it matter now?'

I shake my head and look down at the drawings.

There is music in this house, the kind that pushes gently against the outlines of my body and makes me sway this way and that. Wadih has brought the old stereo player with him from the city and plays our favourite records in the same progression again and again every evening until I find order in anticipation and am strangely comforted.

While Wadih and the men he has hired work on the house in preparation for our child's birth, I lie on the terrace sofa, notebook in hand and a humming between my lips. I have taken to making small illustrations in the page margins, butterflies, shining suns, flowers and geometric shapes in the same pattern as the tiles, which I fill in with the colours Wadih keeps on his desk. He is amused by the childlike drawings, though he does not ask to read the words that lie alongside them.

Occasionally, whenever Selma comes to sit outside with me and to shake her head at the noise the workers are making, she inquires about the contents of the notebook.

'Just my thoughts, Selma,' I reassure her. 'Nothing important.'

Each time she seems satisfied with my answer. 'I've never been one for reading, anyway.'

I feel a sudden inexplicable envy at the freedom implied in her words.

Despite the heat, there is a slight breeze blowing across the terrace when Wadih comes out to join me. I pull up my legs to make room for him to sit down and feel the baby kick through my skin and against my knees.

'She's very active today.' I smile at my husband and rub my belly.

'You're going to have a real shock if it ends up being a boy,' Wadih says and ruffles my hair.

I shrug my shoulders and reach for the notebook.

'Still writing?'

I nod. 'About my mother this time.'

'But your mother never lived here,' Wadih says.

'No, but this is where they met, isn't it?'

I can almost swear to having heard Adel's and Leila's voices murmuring along with mine on lonely nights in this house, but I do not mention this to Wadih.

'What are you going to do with it when you're done?' he asks, pointing at the notebook.

'I don't know. Read the stories to our child perhaps.'

'Yasmeena,' Wadih says in an uncertain voice. He lifts my legs and lays them in his lap.

'Yasmeena,' I call into the breeze. 'Yasmeena.'

LEILA

Leila first noticed the pointed arches that framed the front of the house and thought how lovely a creeping vine would look on them, green and luscious in spring, red and gold in autumn. As it was, the outside of the house looked bare, the jagged white stone and neat red roof almost forbidding. But inside it was different. Signs of home and family were in the fading, comfortable furniture, in the slightly scuffed tile floors and the settled air beneath high ceilings. In the living room a shaft of sunlight came through the large picture windows that overlooked the village souq where Leila could make out small figures moving in and out of the shops and along the street.

Leila, her sister Randa and their parents Nadia and Mahmoud were ushered to their seats by Alia, a moon-faced woman in a loose-fitting long black skirt and top with a diaphanous white veil hanging over her shoulders. Leila felt an accustomed shyness steal its way into her chest and move up into her face. She held her head down and tried to shake the feeling away.

'Welcome to you all. *Ahlan, Ahlan*,' Alia said.

They seated themselves around the room, the young women on the sofa and their parents in armchairs near the door. Alia spoke in clear, rounded tones, her white hands placed neatly on her knees as she sat on the edge of a high-backed chair. Leila shifted in her seat and stared at the older woman, unable to understand what she was saying.

'She's lovely-looking, isn't she, for a woman her age?' Randa whispered into Leila's ear.

Since their arrival from America two months before, the young women had given up trying to understand the language their parents had grown up with and which they had neglected to pass on to them. As Alia and their parents conversed, Leila and Randa could only smile back.

It was not the first time they felt out of place in a country they had heard referred to since childhood as 'back home'. Back home was where fragrant pine trees grew into tall umbrellas and rivers chimed down to a light-blue sea. Back home were snowy winters and balmy summers, and gentle sunshine everywhere in between. There were sandy beaches and mountains where houses perched as if on a breath of air, and people with sing-song greetings of 'how are you', 'God be with you' and 'you have honoured our house with your presence', at every turn.

But everywhere the little girls had looked in the green, leafy fields of West Virginia where they lived, in the small stucco house that met them on their return from school each day and the sharp, clear sound of the English they spoke with their friends was a home without memories, without a stirring, weighted past. They learned to let their minds wander whenever their parents' conversations turned to Arabic, until the words they no longer strained to understand stumbled over one another and became one long tune that lulled them into a secret comfort.

She felt Randa nudge her and pull her up.

A tall young man with a high forehead and fine eye-brows was reaching out to shake Leila's hand. '*Bonjour*,' he said, smiling gently at her.

'This is Rasheed, my son,' Alia said with pride in her voice.

The man bent his head gracefully and when he looked up again Leila noticed a scar in the shape of a wide arch just above his left eyebrow. She saw him lift a long, smooth hand and lightly touch the scar, then he looked at Leila and smiled again. '*Je suis désolé, mais je ne parle que le français et l'arabe*,' Rasheed said with a polite laugh. He placed a chair by Mahmoud and began talking to the older man.

Leila looked away. Since their return to the old country she had watched an unsettling joy light up her parents' eyes every time they met relatives they had missed in their thirty-year absence, or whenever they happened upon a once familiar spot. She had felt a resistance build up within her to sharing a similar certainty in a country that she knew could never be home. Now, everything and every-one she encountered had to be approached with caution. Who would ever know? Leila asked the image in the bathroom mirror late at night when everyone who knew her had fallen asleep. Who can sense the fear in my heart? She would stare back at the large brown eyes wide in astonishment, lips mouthing a silent, round 'O', skin lack-luster in the faint light. The next day she would try again to erase suspicion from her memory, smiling when she could and taking delight in sudden moments of clarity, only to feel doubt creeping back into her, an insistent companion. She turned her head to look out the window once again and let sunlight dazzle her eyes until the figures around her faded into a pleasant blur.

'Hello, there, nice to see our long-lost cousins from Virginia at last.' The voice was abrupt, the English heavily accented. He found her hand and shook it hard.

'I'm Adel, Rasheed's brother. How are you?' He took a seat on the arm of the sofa next to Leila, looking at her until she blushed. He was slightly shorter than his brother and equally thin, but unlike Rasheed, Adel was dark and had sharp features. His body was filled with such palpable energy that she felt herself breathless with anticipation.

He spoke quickly, telling her that he had returned home some years before from America, where he had learned his English. He told her how he had loved America for the huge skies, the prairies and the wheat bending with the wind, and had reveled in the freedom of endless roads leading to nowhere, the anonymity of ambition, and then with equal certainty said there had never been any question of his not returning to Lebanon. 'I had to come back home.'

She pictured a tall young man standing against a ship's railing, waving away a carefree existence, leaning home-ward.

'I stopped and asked myself at that moment why I was leaving, why I had been so determined to return,' Adel said quietly. Then he smiled. 'Just before making my way from California to New York to board ship, I spent one night in your uncle's house in Virginia.'

Leila lifted her eyebrows in astonishment.

'There was a picture of you on the mantelpiece in his house. I asked him who you were.'

She remembered. 'He told me about you,' she cried out. 'My uncle told me about you.'

'And now we meet,' said Adel.

Falling in love had been easy after that. They saw each other almost every day when he came to the house she and her family were staying in just above Beirut. After drinking a cup of coffee, he would grab her hand and pull her behind him towards his car and dare her to guess where they were going. 'I'll show you my Lebanon.'

They visited Roman temples, Phoenician ruins and Arab fortresses, ate local delicacies by cascading rivers and watched the sun dip into the Mediterranean before walking hand in hand up and down endless stretches of soft sand. He took her to meet his brothers and their families in Beirut, and introduced her to his only sister, a sad young woman who lived with her aging in-laws.

When Adel asked Leila to marry him, she felt ready to say 'But I want to go home' until she realized she did not know where home was any more and all she could do was nod her consent.

Just before their late-summer wedding, she discovered that their parents had arranged the meeting between them months earlier. 'Did you know about it?' she asked him.

'Does it matter now?'

On her wedding day, several hundred people came to stare at Leila as she stood, silent and lovely in her off-white satin dress. They shook Adel's hand, then crowded onto the terrace, spilling out into the front garden, singing out in celebration and joy. The men formed a large semicircle around the groom, stamped their feet in unison and then, bending forward, shook their shoulders from side to side. They wished upon the two a prosperous future and plenty of sons to see them into old age, and thanked God for what they saw as a most suitable marriage. One or two of them shook their heads in foreboding, saying the young woman was too foreign in her ways, until Alia came within earshot and they had to hold their tongues. Leila stood by the nest of flowers created in one corner of the living room, her long dress the colour of seashells, her eyes straining homewards.

The marriage faltered between bliss and desolation. Adel would leave the third-floor flat they had rented in the central district of Beirut early every morning and Leila would try to busy herself with housework, wiping away the film of dust that had settled itself on surfaces before stepping into the kitchen to make the evening meal. Just before Adel's return from work, she would stand on the bedroom balcony and ponder about the lives of those she saw walking past, thoughts of her parents and sister in Virginia hovering dangerously near. After dinner she and Adel would settle on the living-room sofa, each with a favorite book, and read aloud to one another until sleep nudged them into bed.

In time, Adel achieved the professional success his mother had always predicted for him, taking him from home for longer intervals, demanding his attention even when he was there. They moved to a larger apartment overlooking the sea, Leila feeling the distance from her husband like a tearing at her heart, reminding herself again and again of the ties that bound them together.

Their two children, a boy and a girl they named Kamal and Maysa, grew so close to the blueness of the Mediterranean that their eyes developed forever looking outward to further horizons. Their mother told them stories of fairies and goblins, princesses running through forests of fir, where birds interrupted silence with song. They understood their faith as that in life itself, and for friends had divided children like themselves who accepted them just as they were.

In their childhood there were tree houses and piles of sand to play in, and a shining, translucent Beirut. Within them was an underlying strength that their parents unknowingly harboured. On Sundays they would sit in the back of the car, their father driving, their mother sitting neatly in the passenger seat beside him, and open the windows all the way, staring at the changing scenery, waiting for that distinct moment when a sudden rush of crisp mountain air blew into their faces. Once at their grandmother's, the children would go into the house and receive hugs and kisses of welcome patiently, before running out again to listen to their footsteps echo among the tall pines that shaded them. And when their aunt Saeeda came out to call them in to lunch, the children would fold away their wings and skip across the terrace, through the front door of the house and into calmness.

Maysa and Kamal, images of their parents' longings, unashamed in the intensity of their love for one another. Leila would touch the tops of their heads and bend down to kiss them before they went off to school in the morning, silently calling to them to stay safe. She knew they missed their father more than they dared say and she tried hard to fill the spaces that he left behind.

Whenever Adel was due back from a trip, Leila would buy small gifts for the children which he gratefully gave them before turning away with exhaustion. And on the night he was late coming home, she would snuggle up into their beds and whisper stories into their ears until the echo of her voice lulled them into a still sleep.

When Adel came back one day with a small camera that took instant pictures with one click of a tiny button, Leila began to carry it in her purse on their Sunday visits to the mountains and would pull it out to photograph the family as they laughed, ate, played, talked and shook their heads at her. 'Leila, put that away and come and eat.' But she would refuse to put the camera down until the photo had been taken.

One particularly brilliant Sunday, the children had managed to drag their father out into the garden after lunch and were trying to persuade him to play with them. Leila grabbed the camera and went after them.

'Please, Daddy, please,' Kamal and Maysa begged Adel. 'Just a short game. Make us fly in circles.'

'I want to have a nap,' Adel told them.

'We'll show you how to play, Daddy. Just for a little while, please.'

Leila watched as they each clasped both hands around one of his and urged him on. 'All you have to do is pull us round, like this,' Maysa said. 'See? It's very easy.' Then she started to sashay round, gently pushing her brother along until all three began to move in circles, Adel around himself and the two children around him. Leila saw him lean further back, his feet moving in a quick gallop, the children bright as stars around him. Dropping the camera on the ground, she knew that at that moment she loved him more than she ever would.

Alia fell ill while Adel was on a business trip to America. Leila telephoned to tell him, the quiet whooshing sound of distance behind her voice making it falter.

'Is it bad?' he asked her and, when she did not answer, added, 'I'll be there soon.'

When he arrived two nights later, Leila was waiting for him in the mountain house with Saeeda and his three brothers and their wives. She opened the door and reached out for him, feeling a measure of her longing satisfied with the brief embrace. Then he pulled away and walked inside. 'How is she?' he asked Rasheed.

'You'd best go in and see her, Adel. The doctor's just been.'

When he came out of the bedroom, Adel's handsome face looked sunken and gray. Leila fetched him a glass of hot tea and urged him to sit down.

'Let's go out onto the terrace,' he said, taking the glass in one hand and leading her out into the chilly night with the other.

He told her he could remember when he was very little how his father would lift him in his arms and wrap him against the chill inside his woolen greatcoat until little Adel felt he was at the center of the world. 'Then, just as I began to fall asleep, Mother would take me from my father's arms, shush away his protests, and carry me into the bedroom where my brothers were preparing to sleep,' Adel continued. 'It was always Rasheed who tucked me into the bed we shared.'

Leila wrapped her arms round herself.

'All those years, I only ever saw her cry once,' Adel said.

'She is strong, Adel. You inherited that strength.'

The night stretched into a fanfare of stars that shone against the outline of trees and distant mountains.

'It was the night after Salam and Rasheed were nearly killed in that accident at the school.'

Leila nodded.

'She came into our bedroom thinking we were all fast asleep and I saw her lean over and place her hand on Rasheed's head as he slept. She kept it there a long time.' Adel gripped the balustrade, the sorrow in his face receding into the darkness, and Leila knew she was alone again.

Moments later they heard a cry coming from the house and rushed inside, their hands clasped tightly together.

MAYSA

The baby will be born today, I am certain. I feel a restlessness that will not leave me and my back aches so that I am unable to sit in a comfortable position. Wadih has gone to find Selma and the doctor, and for a short while at least I am alone.

I pace through the rooms of this house, saying a prayer under my breath, and wait for Alia's spirit to stir in me. The night she died, Kamal and I were sleeping in the back room with our cousins while our parents kept vigil at her bedside. I was somewhere between child and woman, feeling the same anxiety the adults did but not knowing what to do with it. I remember hearing my aunt Saeeda's yell and then the sound of running feet. I rose from my bed and stepped out of the room.

The adults were all crowded around my grandmother's bed and someone was sobbing loudly. I went up to my mother and pulled at her sleeve. She turned with a look of surprise, put her arm round me and pushed me forward towards the bed. Alia was lying perfectly still. Her eyes were closed, her lips shut in a thin long line. Her hands were crossed high on her chest and I noticed that the vein in one of them was a deep, prominent blue and wove up towards her arm like an errant vine.

I brought my hand to my mouth. 'Oh!' I felt my

mother tighten her grip on my shoulder.

But Alia is not to be found. I start to think that I have left too pronounced a mark on this house, so that its past is fading to make way for newer memories. My whole body begins to tremble and I rush to lie on my grandmother's bed. The ceiling seems higher than I remember it and I feel as though I am sinking into the depths of the mattress, further and further, my limbs, head and torso making indentations in the fabric.

I make a fist with my hand and press hard. Here, I suddenly think through the pain, is where I will carry all the wandering recollections, all the thoughts that have been and the people who vanished with them; here, in a tight ball that only I can release. And years from now, whenever someone looks into the wrinkles and crevices that line the surface of my open palm, they will say, 'I see great reserves of strength in you, a coming together of a host of spirits.'

'Maysa.' It is Selma's reassuring voice. 'Maysa,' she says again, her voice hovering above me. 'I'm here now, dear. I'm here.'

I let out a sigh of relief. 'My water just broke, Selma. She is coming now.'

MAYSA

My daughter says she is making a life of her own. Just turned sixteen, she is strong-willed and heartbreakingly beautiful, and from the city apartment she has lived in with her father for the past three months asks me to visit her. 'For once, Mother,' Yasmeena says over the telephone, 'just this once, come into my world.'

But I have been made more stubborn by time and continue to stand at the doorstep of our mountain home, anticipating her return, looking for a glimpse of her endless grace approaching in the distance.

Yasmeena writes me long, drawn-out letters whose language reflects a mixture of simplicity and arrogance. 'Beirut glistens these days, Mother,' she writes. 'People say that now the war is over it will soon regain its former splendor. How long is it since you last saw it? How much longer until you do?'

She tells me that at her request her father has painted the walls of her room a bright yellow and has placed a huge armchair by her bedroom window where she sits 'dreaming and drinking strong black coffee' before making her way to school every morning.

'You will be happy to hear that Father and I get on well, but then I had expected that. During the day he works on his designs in the study and only comes out in the evening to make our supper. You should see him. He holds his breath until I take the first mouthful of whatever he has created and smiles when I nod my approval. It's quite touching, really, I mean to see a man trying so hard to please.

We speak of you often, Mother, and wish you would come to spend a few weeks with us next spring. Will you?

The years run away from me. It seems not so long ago that Yasmeena rested on my hip as I carried her and walked through our garden. She would tip herself forward in my arms to reach for something on the ground and I would lean with her, our bodies straining against one another in motion. When she grew too heavy for me to carry, my daughter pressed herself against my legs as we walked, only letting go to scurry uncertainly towards her father or some other fleeting longing.

'You crowd her,' Wadih often told me.

And I would gently push Yasmeena away from me and watch a look of anxious surprise appear on her face. 'Go on, sweetheart,' I would say to my child, my heart taking a leap. 'Go outside and play.'

At bedtime, while Wadih worked in the living room, Yasmeena and I would lie on her bed with the notebook between us. She would open it to a page of her choice and ask me to tell her that day's story, tales of near love and certain loss attached firmly to the names of her ancestors.

'Was Great-grandmother brave and strong, Mama?' she would ask in her baby voice. 'Was she like the two of us together?'

After she fell asleep, I would dare to lift my daughter into my arms and bury my face in her fragrant neck. I cannot remember what I whispered to her in those dark hours, nor if she ever woke to the sound of my voice, but I will not forget how it felt to hold her, the heat from her small body warming me, gleaming between us like gold dust.

For her first day at the village school Yasmeena wore a blue dress Selma made for the occasion and had her long black hair tied back with a white bow. She was unusually silent through our preparations and my nervous chatter. When she was ready, her father took her hand and they walked out of the door with me in their wake.

'Daddy will be back to pick you up as soon as you're done, darling,' I tried to reassure her.

Yasmeena stopped to look back at me, then lifted her free hand above her head and held it there for a moment. But before I could move towards her, Wadih was pulling her gently to the car. She did not look back again.

I remember leaning against the green balustrade on one side of the terrace to watch the car moving away towards the village high street, Yasmeena's little head just visible in the front passenger seat, Wadih adjusting the left view mirror as he drove. For a moment my heart raced away with them, until the car disappeared from sight and I could turn once again to my house for solace.

★

What am I to do with skin touched by years on this mountain that has made me a mere outline of the surrounding air? Shall I wrap it in a tight bundle and leave it on this doorstep before I leave, or send it flying through the trees like a bird with nowhere to go? I have felt time sink into me, spread through my body and disguise itself in a thousand different ways. Now I long for escape.

I dreamed I saw my whole life: people past and present and those who have been with me standing against a background of green. There was certainty in those encounters, love for my life's companions unceasing and already in my heart before our meeting.

Mountain people have long believed in the undying spirit, in lives that are like sea waves, coming and then pulling back. As a child, I remember hearing of loved ones who had died being declared reborn in faraway places, and watched as veiled women and bearded sheikhs climbed into cars and drove away to find and question the miracle children. Sometimes the incarnations were closer to home, four-year-old cousins recounting their stories, the circumstances of their deaths and the families they'd once had.

This belief in reincarnation does not reassure us of the existence of an afterlife, nor does it mean the single repetition of joys and hardships. Rather, it shows us the vital part we play in the infinite process of living, the uninterrupted movement towards oneness. I ask this house where Alia's spirit is now. Did it find another body to inhabit after her passing or is the trembling I have felt merely her soul's shadow, colliding with mine, drawing stars onto my skin and, for an instant, making me ethereal too?

Wadih stayed with us until the day after Yasmeena's seventh birthday. He woke early that morning, packed a stack of design drawings into his large leather folder and came to sit by me on the bed. 'It's time I left,' he began.

I shook my head.

'You don't need me any more and I want to return to the city.'

'Yasmeena needs you,' I protested.

'But you don't, Maysa.'

I turned away from him to bury my face in the pillow and remained silent until he got up and left.

I spent that first night feeling as though I were missing someone I already held in my arms. Yasmeena sensed my anxiety and asked for her father again and again. A week after his departure, I telephoned Wadih at our old apartment and asked him to tell his daughter what had happened. 'It's not as easy to run away from a child, Wadih. You'll have to give her some sort of explanation.'

'I ran away?' I heard the astonishment in his voice before I handed Yasmeena the receiver.

He spoke to her for a long time. She nodded her head several times and finally: 'Yes, Daddy. I love you too.'

My young daughter's hug was especially close that bedtime. Once she had let go of me, she reached up and stroked my hair. 'You can take me to school now,

Mummy,' she said. 'He'll always be thinking of us, Mummy. He said so.'

When I reached for the notebook and handed it to Yasmeena to choose a bedtime story, she shook her head and mouthed a silent 'no'. 'They're in my head, Mama. All the stories are already in my head,' she repeated before snuggling into the bed and closing her eyes.

I got up and placed the notebook in a drawer in my clothes cupboard, where it stayed throughout Yasmeena's childhood.

Wadih came to visit us over the years, arriving on our doorstep, his arms laden with presents for Yasmeena and me. She would squeal with excitement at seeing him, guide him into the living room and then jump into his lap as soon as he sat down. 'What did you bring me this time, Daddy? Is there something for Mummy too?'

On school holidays, Wadih came for Yasmeena and took her away for a week or two at a time. When they returned, I would search their faces for signs of discontent and feel a momentary disappointment at its absence. 'Were you happy?' I would ask my daughter as I held her close.

'Yes. Yes. Yes.' She would laugh and nod at her father.

'I'm glad, my darling,' I whispered into her ear. 'So glad.'

Wadih and I did not speak of his departure, preferring instead to make Yasmeena our topic of conversation. We had long telephone conversations during which we discussed everything from her schooling to the length of her hair, and whenever he came for a visit we would sit on my terrace and chat companionably about the wonder of her. Yasmeena was the center of our separate worlds and on the surface we were good at sharing her.

I have kept myself busy since my daughter's departure. My house is unrelenting in its demands for my attention and the garden waits for me every evening like an impatient lover. It is work that is never done and belongs to me, as it did to my grandmother long before me.

Painting a rickety shelf or mending a curtain hem, I wonder if Alia taught herself, as I have, to dwell on the details of daily life, to know in these moments her soul's longings. Did she see herself in the inevitable loneliness of always being half-wife, half-mother and never entirely herself? I kneel on the kitchen floor and scrub the beautiful arabesque tiles that are chipped and faded with time and wandering feet, and remember that my daughter was once like this with me, her little body tense with the joy of labour.

Selma visits me several times a week. She carries herself like a proud old woman now, her back straight and the white veil she now insists on wearing draped loosely over her wide shoulders. She has not been formally initiated into the religion yet but tells me that ever since she turned sixty several months ago she has been thinking seriously about it.

'So what exactly are you waiting for?' I ask her in a gentle, mocking tone.

'Time.'

'Time?'

'The right moment,' Selma replies, impatient. 'You're laughing at me and I'm not prepared to talk about it if you can't take me seriously.'

I shake my head and lean over to pat her affectionately on the knee. 'You know I love you, Selma. You know that, don't you?'

She stands up. 'You can't understand, can you, needing to have faith in something after all these long, difficult years?'

She is right. I find it difficult to accept that someone as wise as my Selma should feel such a need.

I see our faith in the colours and scents that fill this mountain, in the quiet green of pine and the peppery fragrance of prickly bush; in the translucent whites and insistent black worn by religious initiates; in the rich smells of trampled earth beneath the feet of running children; and perhaps most of all in the memories my grandmother left behind, the legacy of stars.

Selma wants me to accompany her to one of the Thursday night prayer meetings that she now regularly attends. 'I'm not asking you to turn religious,' she retorts when I express reluctance. 'Just come with me this once, that's all.'

'You think I'm lonely now that Yasmeena is gone, don't you? You think I need to be kept entertained.'

'Oh, suit yourself.'

I finally go with her anyway because I know I will never hear the end of it if I don't. I even agree to wear a veil, although I do not place it on my head until we are just outside the prayer room where dozens of pairs of shoes are lined up in neat rows.

Inside, the women are sitting cross-legged on the floor on one side of the room, quietly muttering to themselves. From the other side of the curtain that divides the room in half there is the murmur of deep male voices.

Selma pulls me down to the floor beside her and places her finger across her lips. 'Listen now,' she whispers.

Everyone goes quiet. From where I am sitting I can feel an evening breeze fly through the window and sway the dividing curtain. A woman behind me sighs deeply and fidgets slightly. I steal a glance at Selma. Her head is bowed and her eyes are closed. In profile, with the white veil framing her face, her features look softer, more vulnerable. I reach out to touch her but before I can a man's voice begins to recite the opening prayer and all the initiates follow suit.

'In the name of God,' I begin, following the movements of the women round me, then end the prayer, as is customary, by sweeping both hands across and down my face as though I were washing it.

The male voice begins again.

'Who is that talking?' I ask Selma.

'He's not talking, he's reciting,' she whispers back. 'It's Sheikh Salman, the Blue Sheikh.'

'Blue?'

'The head Sheikh. He wears blue robes instead of black. Just repeat after him like the rest of us.'

I listen to the quiet murmuring around me and think of the rows of shoes by the doorstep outside, and the path to my house beyond them. I feel my shoulders sinking into my chest and reach up to rub my neck. The voices begin to melt into one another and I can no longer hear the individual words. The breeze returns and pushes the veil off my head. No one notices, they are too absorbed in their chanting. I sigh and listen to all the languages of the world, one infinite melody of space and distance. I feel my breath float before me and touch Selma's face, then drift again towards the other women and to the men behind the trembling curtain.

'Maysa, Maysa,' I hear Selma calling softly. 'You're crying. Why are you crying?'

I go to the prayer meeting with Selma every Thursday. She arrives at my doorstep flustered with everyday anxieties until we make our way to the prayer room with a lightness in our step. My long white veil has become my most prized article of clothing, diaphanous and woven with light, and as soon as I put it on my mind no longer attempts to wander.

I am now a familiar sight to my praying companions and though they do not entirely embrace me as one of them, they never object to my presence.

'We'll have to tell them soon,' Selma says to me one day as we walk to the prayer room.

'Tell them what?'

'Why you've been coming to the meetings lately.'

I stop and look at her. 'But I don't even know why,' I protest.

'I know that.'

Perhaps it is the silence between the sacred words as they are repeated again and again, unquestioned by the men and women who recite them, ubiquitous as air. Perhaps it is the sense of companionship, the assurance that in this place at least my presence requires no justification.

Or maybe it is those shoes outside the door, waiting as if resigned to their fate and always there when we come out and the setting sun beckons us home.

A few days after my exchange with Selma, Yasmeena asked me once again to come and see her. This time I agreed.

'It's Father,' my daughter began over the telephone. 'I don't know what's the matter with him. He's stopped going to work and mopes round the house all the time. I don't know what to do, Mama.'

'Has something happened?' I question her. 'Have you asked him?'

'He won't talk to me,' she replied, her voice straining slightly. 'Please, Mother, I need you here to help me with him.'

'I'll be there tomorrow afternoon.'

★

Early evening and I am sitting on my bed imagining flight. Selma has been and gone, leaving a trace of regret behind. When I told her I would be going to the city tomorrow she smiled so enthusiastically that I could not help but show my anger. 'You want me to leave?' I asked.

'Your place is with your husband and child.'

'I'm tired of you telling me what I should and should not do, Selma.'

She nodded and leaned forward to plant a kiss on my cheek. 'Go with God,' she said.

I get up and open my clothes cupboard. I will pack a few things in case I decide to stay in Beirut for a few days. I place trousers, tops and underwear in an overnight bag and then find myself reaching into the top drawer. Inside is the old notebook that Yasmeena rejected all those years ago. I pick it up and put it into the bag.

Beirut is a recurring dream, at once elusive and familiar, a keepsake of a drifting mind. Blue sea, beeping car horns, fishmongers and vegetable carts, dust, people calling to one another from balconies, sun, noise and an insistent sense of ordered confusion. I arrive early and decide to sit in a café on the beach before making my way to Wadih's apartment.

In May the sky and water here appear in collusion, both a brilliant blue, both unruffled. Sipping the thick and bitter Arabic coffee, I adjust my eyes to the even nature of the view. When I turn my head I can see the hills above Beirut. As a child, this was a vision that greeted me every morning, water on one side of me and mountains on the other. I am reassured by it now as I was then and when I get up to go I know that I will be able to offer solace to my troubled husband.

'Wadih, you look tired.' I'm standing on his doorstep, shocked at the drooping contours of his face.

'Maysa.' He motions for me to come in. 'Yasmeena is still at school.'

'Yes, I know. Will you make me some tea?'

The apartment is uncluttered. I see Wadih's touch in its spareness, functional pieces outlined in space. He leads me to a dark-green sofa that is pushed back against the white living-room wall. There is a glass coffee table in front of it and a squat off-white lamp on the floor by its side. The windows are curtainless and there is no sign of Yasmeena's happy clutter here.

'Her room is different,' Wadih says and places the tea tray on the glass table.

I nod and begin to pour the tea. 'Is Yasmeena all right?' I ask him.

'I think she's worrying a little too much about me these days.'

'She must have good reason to. Is your work not going well, Wadih?' Even as I ask the question, I can feel him going into one of his long silences. For a brief moment we sip away at our tea and look away from each other.

My eyes drift to the other side of the room. Wadih's work table is in the corner adjacent to the window. It is uncharacteristically untidy and piled high with books, reams of paper and plastic colored trays. I place my teacup on the tray and get up. 'Are you working on something at the moment?' I ask Wadih as I make my way to the work table.

In the midst of the disorder is a charcoal drawing of a woman. She is leaning down on one knee, looking out at what appears to be a sea of shoes that have been placed in neat rows all around her. The woman's head is partially covered with a long veil that falls over the curve of one shoulder. Her features are not clearly defined but the look of confident rapture on her face is unmistakable. I reach out to touch her face. 'That's me,' I say quietly.

I hear Wadih come up behind me. 'No. That's a drawing of Selma.'

I draw in my breath.

'I went up to the mountain to see you several weeks ago and when I got to the village they told me you were at the prayer meeting. I walked up there and waited for you outside, and eventually saw Selma come out and put on her shoes.' He places a hand on my shoulder. 'I didn't know you had become interested in religion,' Wadih continues.

'You didn't wait to talk to me.'

'I was afraid I'd see the same look on your face that I had seen in Selma's.' He pulls away from me and I am suddenly aware of the gap between our bodies as if it would swallow me into it.

His voice floats over my shoulder. 'She seems so complete on her own, doesn't she?' he says. 'She really belongs there.'

I nod in agreement and turn round to face him. My own attempts at belonging have always seemed half-hearted to me, a kind of unconvincing recognition of a universal need that slips from me whenever I attempt to embrace it.

I move to the sofa, open the overnight bag and pull out the old notebook.

'Your story,' Wadih says quietly.

'Alia's, not mine.'

'Is there a difference?'

He comes up to me and I notice that his eyes have not faded with age; they seem darker somehow and are framed with thicker lashes than I remember.

'I brought this for Yasmeena,' I say with a shrug. 'I thought she might want to look at it again after all these years.'

'She knows who she is, Maysa. Don't confuse the child.'

I hold out the notebook to him. 'These are the stories of the women in our family. She needs to know . . .'

'These!' Wadih says, snatching the notebook from me. 'These are the stories you have been telling yourself because you are unable to embrace your own.'

I have not heard Wadih raise his voice in a long time and I am startled into a breathless silence. I stare at him and, for one moment, his face seems to glow in the afternoon light.

'The last time I tried to read it to her was the night you left the mountain,' I tell him. 'She told me she already knew all the stories by heart and I just put the notebook away in a cupboard.'

'Have you had enough of the mountain now?' Wadih's voice is strained.

'What do you mean?'

'I'm asking you if you think you're ready to come back to us, Maysa.'

I step forward and place my head on his shoulder. I wonder at the choices I have made, at this constant pull between the places and people I have loved. I breathe in the scent of Wadih's skin. When I close my eyes and feel his arms round me, I see an image of my house encircled in shadow. 'How did you know?' I ask Wadih. 'Just how did you know?'

PART II

Aida decided from a very young age to cling to childhood, so that when she eventually found herself moving inexorably towards maturity, remnants of that earlier reluctance had already fixed themselves to her every aspect.

Her fair hair folded itself round her head in soft thin waves and her face remained perfectly round, dominated by a pair of large eyes that suggested melancholy rather than wisdom. Her height was unimpressive and her demeanour hesitant.

But what Aida lacked in physical attributes, she made up for in creative thinking. She had a near-perfect memory for the minutiae of her past, for the measureless variety of passions that had once filled her days. Sitting in the clipped quietness of her room, she would shift her mind into recollections of home until the images appeared, layers of moment piled on top of each other, searchlights into history.

There were people and mysteries in her story, and a perception of time that gave Beirut a flavor of endlessness. In her mind's eye she saw the sea, a soft, blue Mediterranean, and smelled the air that floated above it, a mixture of hope and God's breezes. She recalled the sounds that had once greeted her mornings, voices and places and the unrelenting hum of activity, so that even now, whenever silence came after her, echoes of a home long gone would rush into Aida's ears and fill her heart.

Amou Mohammed's hollow rubber slippers made a plopping sound as he made his way down the marble steps of the building's entrance. Aida watched him sweep Beirut's morning dust back and forth with his broom into an ever-growing pile. When he had reached the pavement, he looked up at her and smiled. She skipped down to him, the hem of her school dress chafing against her legs, grabbed the broom and began gently to swing it back and forth, mimicking his graceful movements. She swept and swept and watched the tiny specks of dust settle into the crevices of the pavement tiles and float out onto the streets where hooting cars and crowded buses trampled them unwittingly.

Around her, the day had begun its rhythmic jostling match of people and machines, of incessant noise and the heady scents of city life. She stood perfectly still, gripped the broom handle a little harder and closed her eyes. She felt a hand resting gently on her shoulder.

'Good job, Aida,' Amou Mohammed said quietly. 'Well done.'

Moments later, her two sisters stepped out of the lift at the top of the steps and ran down to wait for the school bus with her. Aida handed the broom back to Amou Mohammed and turned to them.

'You came down without telling us,' chided Sara, Aida's older sister.

Dina, the youngest of the three, began chattering away as she always did in the mornings and Aida was saved from replying with a suitable excuse.

As soon as the school bus arrived, the three girls lifted their heads and waved to their mother who was standing on the balcony of their fifth-floor apartment. Amou Mohammed helped them onto the bus. Looking out of the window as the bus began to move away, Aida thought she saw him wink at her.

The cities of the West became her refuge. She walked their streets with confidence, slipping myriad cultures into her pockets and learning how to smile in several languages. She was faceless one moment and shining the next, and in her manner no secrets were revealed.

There were more friends than lovers in Aida's adult life, although neither lasted very long for Beirut was always there, in sidelong glimpses and sudden movements, so that she had no heart to waste on new beginnings.

Sometimes her strength would leave her and she would find herself feeling unexpected joy at a golden autumn or summer rain, or in the kindness of strangers with coloured eyes. For a moment confusion would sweep over her until she gathered herself together once again and remembered all the things she had left behind.

When civil war broke out in Lebanon, Aida was seventeen and in high school. The family, Aida's parents, her two sisters and herself, made a decision to leave soon after the first battle for Ras Beirut ripped through their complacency. They packed a suitcase each and piled into two large taxis for the short drive to the city's beleaguered airport.

Amou Mohammed was there to see them off. He hugged the three girls and shook hands with their parents. Then he lifted both his hands above his head and waved to the cars as they drove away. Aida put her head out the window and shouted to him. 'I'll be back, Amou Mohammed. I promise I'll be back.'

Once accustomed to the isolation in her new life, Aida grew to love the vast parks of Europe after rain, when a hundred shades of green lit the pathways beneath her feet and glistened in the trees above her head. Dressed in a long grey raincoat that she tied tightly round her waist and with her hands thrust deep into her pockets, she would walk for hours, watching for solitude.

On the day she heard of Amou Mohammed's death she put down the phone, donned her raincoat and rushed to a nearby park. Her breath came out in bursts as she walked and there was an insistent ringing in her ears.

The memories came back quickly and stumbled over each other: his delight in loving, his gentleness and the lilt in his voice whenever he came to the end of a story he had been telling her. She remembered him standing at the top of the steps that led to their building, one hand on his waist, the other shading his eyes as he looked out to sea. She saw the stoop in his shoulders as he swept with his broom and the droplet of spit that sometimes rested on his lower lip when he spoke, stretching itself upwards with his words.

And all the while Aida waded through the dust of her past, she refused to see the look of astonishment on Amou Mohammed's beautiful face as the militiaman pointed the rifle to his head and pulled the trigger.

If Aida was a shy child it was because the world seemed so mysterious to her that only stillness could unfold it. Whenever people came to visit she would hide behind the living-room door and peek at them at intervals, until Mother called her to come in and 'say hello'. Aida would traipse in after her sisters and endure the kisses and handshaking of well-meaning adults. She especially dreaded being asked questions – how old are you? What class are you in – and would hang her head as she muttered reluctant replies.

Sometimes, surrounded by an unending supply of extended-family members, Aida would feel herself being absorbed into them until she disappeared into their smiles and caresses, and could no longer tell where she began and where they ended. She became everyone she had ever known. She was the distant cousin who sat in the living room, wrapping his roughened hand round a small Arabic coffee cup, making a noise as he sipped at the bitter liquid. She was Mother on a night out, dressed in red silk and smelling of flowers, or Father arriving from the office, his sudden masculine presence filling the apartment until the evening seemed more sharp-edged and replete with possibility.

Sometimes she became the city itself during those moments when sun and shadow met on doorsteps, framing everyone in incandescence so that they seemed to draw beauty with their fingertips. And if she stretched her imagination far enough she could see into the future, to a time when Beirut's eyes shed tears of regret.

She saw him the first time as she sat on a park bench one crisp November afternoon. She had been there for a while, looking out at a vast pond that reflected light onto the bare trees.

'Aida, Aida,' Amou Mohammed said quietly and then laughed. 'Do you remember me?' She could not bring herself to speak. She turned to look at him, his handsome face and slim frame breathing beside her, and simply shook her head. They sat together until the sun began to fade and before he left he asked her, 'When are you coming home?'

On most days Amou Mohammed ate his midday meal in the family kitchen. He sat on a low stool at a Formica table that had been pushed back against the wall, his long legs bent, his arms almost reaching the floor. Leaning forward, he would tear off pieces of flat Arabic bread to scoop up the stew and rice that mother had placed in a plate before him. And when the girls had finished their own lunch in the dining room, they would file into the kitchen to watch Amou Mohammed eat.

'Is it good?' Dina pushed Aida out of the way and stood

directly in front of Amou Mohammed.

'Very.'

Aida reached into the bread box. 'Here, have some more bread,' she said, handing him another loaf.

Then Sara came up behind the two younger girls. 'Can we go downstairs with you when you've finished eating?'

'Girls, leave Amou Mohammed alone,' Mother said as she came into the kitchen. 'Let him eat in peace.'

Amou Mohammed looked up at her and smiled. Mother shook her head and walked out again with a basket of fruit.

Aida leaned against Amou Mohammed's shoulder and felt the sharpness in his bones. 'Can I get you more bread, Amou Mohammed?' she asked him.

He shook his head and chewed his food slowly.

'Mother said to leave him alone.' Dina sidled up to Aida and started to fidget.

Amou Mohammed reached out and put his arm round both of them. He had stopped chewing. '*Yalla*, I'm done,' he told the girls. 'We can go now.' He got up and put his plate in the sink. After he had washed his hands, he turned to the children. 'Are you all ready?'

Dina began to jump up and down, and Sara rushed to the front door.

Aida took Amou Mohammed's hand and looked up at him. 'Why don't you ever eat with us in the dining room, Amou Mohammed?'

He squeezed her hand and led her out of the kitchen.

★

The second time Aida was standing outside a school play-ground watching children weaving themselves through winter sunlight.

Suddenly, he was next to her, shuffling his feet on the pavement. 'I used to watch over you like this when you were children,' he said. 'Do you remember, Aida?'

Sara had dared her sisters to climb over the concrete wall that separated their building from the one next door. She piled several wooden crates up against the wall, scrambled up them and reached for the narrow ledge above. Pulling herself up with her thin arms, she was suddenly standing on top of the wall, looking down at Aida and Dina with a big grin. 'Come on, you two,' she called down to them, 'don't chicken out now.' Then she disappeared over the other side.

Aida knew she had no choice but to follow. Her heart beat hard against her chest as she began the slow climb up the boxes, scraping her knee as she did so. She heaved herself up onto the ledge and tried to stand up as Sara had done but when she looked down and realized how far away the ground was she began to panic. Her eyes, as they always did at such moments, betrayed her and she began to cry.

'Just put one leg over the wall and sit down,' Sara told her. 'Don't be scared, Aida, you'll be all right.'

Aida followed her sister's advice. 'What do I do now?'

'Dina, go get Amou Mohammed,' Sara called to their younger sister. 'Hurry up, tell him there's an emergency.'

When Amou Mohammed arrived a few minutes later,

Aida was still sitting on the wall and the tears hadn't stopped. She saw him look up at her and immediately hung her head, shame sweeping through her until her whole body shook with it.

'Hey, Aida,' said Amou Mohammed. She could hear quiet laughter in his voice. 'What have you done now?' Then she heard him push the boxes away. 'I'm standing right underneath you. All you have to do is swing your leg over and jump.'

Aida shook her head and Amou Mohammed chuckled.

She swallowed down her humiliation and looked at him. His long arms were reaching for her. At that moment her sisters, who stood close by, seemed everything that she was not, brave and bright and solid against the frame of morning light.

Aida took a deep breath, swung her leg over the wall and threw herself into Amou Mohammed's tight grasp. After he had put her down, she turned round and walked away, refusing to look at him.

Suddenly aware of the children's voices in the playground, Aida wrapped her coat more tightly round herself. 'You laughed at me,' she told the ghost lingering beside her.

'You invited laughter.'

'Was it because I was a joke to you?'

'No. It was because you were a joy.'

On the first anniversary of Amou Mohammed's death, the three sisters met at Dina's house. Sara and Dina had changed. Both were married and wore an air of permanence that had so far eluded Aida. Sara practiced medicine in a large hospital and was pregnant with her first child. Dina worked for a recruitment firm and earned a very good salary.

'Have you heard the latest news from home?' Aida asked.

'You mean the type of news that usually begins with "fierce fighting broke out in Beirut"?' Dina replied.

'No, no. I mean there was some kind of ceasefire initiative yesterday. Maybe things will quieten down now.'

Sara shook her head and reached for her coffee cup. Her straight hair shone and fell over her forehead just as it had when she was a child. Aida had to stop herself from leaning over and pushing it off her face.

'I've received another letter from Hisham, Amou Mohammed's eldest son,' Aida said.

'How are they all?' asked Dina.

Amou Mohammed's wife and children had all moved out of the refugee camp that had been their home and now lived and worked in the Gulf.

'They're doing well. Hisham and his brothers have found jobs and they're much better off than they were before. The letter upset me, though.'

'What do you mean?' Dina leaned back on the sofa and put her bare feet up on the coffee table. Her toes were short and squat, just like a child's, and were painted a deep, dark red.

Aida looked up at her sister's face before speaking. 'It was in reply to a letter I sent him months ago. I told him how important his father had been to us. He said we saw more of Amou Mohammed as children than they did.'

The room seemed to turn cold.

Like many other Palestinian refugees who lived in Beirut, Amou Mohammed had spent most of his time at his place of work, visiting his wife and children at the camp on the other side of town only on the occasional Sunday.

'Maybe we should write to Hisham and tell him how bad we feel,' Dina said.

Sara shook her head. 'It wouldn't make any difference. Hisham has a right to feel bitter, but it's too late to do anything about it.'

Dina nodded.

'Anyway,' Sara began again, 'it's not as if Amou Mohammed is really gone.' She hesitated before continuing. 'Not a day goes by when I don't think of him at some point or other . . .' Then she lifted her head and looked towards the mantelpiece. 'Where did you get that photograph?'

Dina stood up, reached for the large silver frame on the mantelpiece and handed it to her sister.

Amou Mohammed sat on the front balcony with their mother. He was smiling and gesturing with one hand while his eyes looked directly at the camera. The contours of his face were open and smooth.

'I found it among Mother's things and had it enlarged,' Dina said.

'He was so handsome,' Sara whispered, handing the photograph back.

Dina gazed at it in silence for a few moments before replacing it on the mantel.

Two weeks before Aida's thirteenth birthday Amou Mohammed decided that Sara and Aida should go with him to visit his family. 'It's about time you found out how poor people live,' he told them.

Aida had been too embarrassed to say she did not want to go and simply nodded at his invitation. In truth, she dreaded the thought of entering the unknown world of refugee camps and poverty, and what she imagined would be total squalor. Amou Mohammed had told her many stories about the home that he and his parents had left behind when they were forced out of Palestine many years before, and she did not want to see the same sorrow in a hundred other pairs of eyes.

On Sunday, the three of them set out just before noon. They walked several blocks to a main road and flagged a *service*, one of the innumerable small Mercedes cars that took passengers to destinations around Beirut for 25 piastres each. The ride was long and uncomfortable, and the car seemed to be going through increasingly shabby streets. Amou Mohammed said nothing, merely turning and smiling at the two girls every once in a while.

'Are we nearly there?' Aida asked ten minutes after they had set off.

Amou Mohammed shook his head. As she looked at

the sharp edges of his profile, Aida thought Amou Mohammed seemed suddenly unfamiliar. It was as if his attention had wandered beyond her and Sara, beyond the building overlooking the sea and the life they shared there. She felt her spirits fall.

Amou Mohammed eventually gestured to the driver to stop and they got out onto a street where dozens of tired-looking buildings leaned against one another and the uneven pavements were covered with dirt. He led the sisters through a labyrinth of similarly crowded and noisy lanes until they came to an alleyway that had small, concrete, one-story structures on either side. 'It's just a few houses down,' said Amou Mohammed.

They walked between the open gutters that ran alongside the path. Barefoot and disheveled children wandered listlessly up and down the alleyway and tugged at Aida's sleeves for attention. The level of noise was unlike any she had ever heard. Aida moved closer to her sister and looked at Amou Mohammed for help but he was already a few steps ahead of them. He walked quickly, with his head held down and his arms swinging in a wide angle at his side.

Moments later he turned a corner and gestured to the two girls to follow him. They stepped into a small courtyard where leafy plants grew out of large tins filled with dirt. The ground had been swept clean and a sudden stillness filled the air. To the right of a low dividing wall Aida noticed a sink and toilet behind a wooden door that had been left slightly ajar. The confusion they had encountered when they first entered the camp seemed very far away.

Aida took a deep breath and whispered in her sister's ear, 'This is it?'

Sara shrugged and gestured towards Amou Mohammed who removed his shoes and placed them to one side of the front door. He asked the girls to do the same. 'This is it,' he said. 'Let's go inside; they're all waiting for us.'

The room was crowded with things and people. Amou Mohammed's children rushed to greet him while his wife stood to one side carrying a baby in her arms. There were large embroidered cushions on the carpeted floor and what was clearly bedding for half a dozen people piled high in one corner. A curtain separated one end of the room from the rest. Although Aida had felt a sudden shaft of light when she first entered, she realized that only one bare light bulb hung from the ceiling.

'Here are Sara and Aida come to see you at last.' Amou Mohammed beamed at his family.

The sisters shook hands with each of the children as Amou Mohammed introduced them. Hisham was the eldest, a tall, slim boy with a dignified demeanor. He greeted them and then moved away to make way for his brother Ahmad and sisters Amal and Huda. Bending down to embrace a little girl with golden hair and bright blue eyes, Amou Mohammed said, 'This is our darling Mayyada. Shake hands with our guests, *habibti*.' The little girl put out a small pale hand and looked up solemnly at Sara and Aida.

'Um Hisham,' Amou Mohammed called to his wife,

'bring the baby here to show the girls.'

Um Hisham handed her bundle to her husband and shook hands with the sisters.

'And this is little Sara,' Amou Mohammed said, tipping the baby slightly so they could see her face.

Aida watched as her sister looked down at the baby with something like wonder. 'This is the one you named after me,' Sara said to Amou Mohammed who nodded gently back.

Sara reached for the baby and held her in her arms. Everyone went suddenly very quiet.

As the children crowded round her, Aida thought she felt the rhythm of their hearts beating against her own chest. Sara looked up at Amou Mohammed and smiled until her face lit up like a star. 'She is my namesake and I am her big sister now.'

Everyone cheered and clapped.

'Come on,' said Amou Mohammed. 'Let's eat.'

They sat in a wide circle on the floor. Um Hisham and her two elder daughters began to place small dishes filled with food in front of them while Hisham handed round loaves of flat bread. Aida heard her hosts quietly recall the name of Allah before breaking off large pieces of bread and scooping up the food.

Sara sat between Hisham and Amal, and was happily talking and eating.

'Aida, what are you waiting for?' Amou Mohammed asked her. 'You'll have to make do without a knife and fork today, my dear.'

Everyone laughed and Aida felt her face go red with shame. She slowly broke off a piece of bread and reached for the dish nearest to her.

When Amou Mohammed finally took them home it was already dark outside. They made the journey back in silence. At the front door of their apartment, Amou Mohammed asked the girls what they had thought of his family.

'It was wonderful,' Sara said, leaning her head against him. 'I had a lovely time.'

'And you, Aida, what did you think?'

'You never told me what you thought of your visit to the refugee camp,' he told her as they sat at a roadside café one afternoon.

Aida looked at him, marveling at the smooth lines of his ageless face. In the fading European light, he had a romantic air about him, a kind of soft shimmering at the edges. 'Sara spoke about the visit a few months after we heard of your death,' she said.

He looked away and into the distance.

'She said that when she walked into your home, she realized you had the ability to turn hell into heaven just by being there.'

A moment later he was gone.

Ras Beirut's heart beat loudest on Hamra Street where the shops on either side spilled onto crowded pavements, wares and people mingling in uninterrupted movement.

On their monthly shopping expeditions to Hamra, Aida clung resolutely to her mother's hand, squeezing it hard whenever the frenetic activity around her appeared to get too close.

'Aida, you're hurting me,' Mother would say at intervals until the little girl finally loosened her grip.

Once they got to their first stop at the international bookshop, the three girls could roam freely while Mother carefully looked through the many books and magazines in English that lined the shelves. Aida would pass her fingers across the backs of the books on the lowest shelf at the front end of the shop and move steadily towards the children's section that occupied a small corner at the back. Once there, she would choose a book, sit cross-legged on the floor and look through it. Sometimes Dina would join her and together they marvelled at illustrations of winged fairies, forests thick with green and wide-eyed children in short pants and Mary Jane shoes.

'Read to me,' Dina would say, pointing to the pictures.

And Aida would shift the book so that it lay squarely between them and begin to tell the story she imagined in the words that lay neatly next to one another on the page. Dina would get so absorbed in the tale her sister was weaving that she would lean her head against Aida's shoulder and rest it there for a while.

Later, when their mother read the same books out loud as the two girls fidgeted in their beds before sleep, Dina would interrupt her with Aida's version of the story. 'But that's not what happened, Mother,' she protested sleepily.

Aida held her breath, waiting for her mother to make some kind of reprimand. Moments later, Mother bent down to hold and kiss their faces, bidding them goodnight.

'Aida, how many stories are there in one book?' Dina asked one day as the two girls sat reading in the bookshop.

Aida fingered the large picture book that lay open on her knees, its weight her comfort, and shrugged her shoulders. 'As many as we like, Dina,' she said after a pause. 'Just as many as we like.'

Aida decided to settle into a kind of life, teaching at a nursery school in a quiet city neighbourhood where trees outnumbered buildings and winters were soaked in melancholy. Her pupils came from all parts of the globe, steeped in the cultures of their ancestors. They held their different-coloured hands before them with the same wonder, shouted out loud with happiness and, whenever loneliness came over them, all sought the solace of friendship.

Aida was surprised at herself for having strong feelings about her pupils, liking or disliking them as she did the adults she encountered, and marvelling at the strength of their personalities, the sureness of their place in the world.

Julian was her star child, a quiet three-year-old boy whose broad face and fair hair reminded her of the stories she had read in childhood. He arrived on the first day of school dressed in woolen gray shorts and a bright red jumper. His dark shoes were immaculately polished and he carried a leather satchel that contained a well-worn colouring book and a variety of blunt crayons.

When Aida asked the children to join her in a circle in the centre of the large classroom, Julian sat down, crossed his stocky legs, placed his hands on his knees and stole glances at the two girls sitting on either side of him.

'Boys and girls,' Aida said, smiling, 'I want to welcome you to your first day at school.'

There were one or two sniffles from those trying to hold back tears. Julian looked straight at his teacher.

'Why don't we start with a song that we all know and then we can introduce ourselves to one another?' Aida began. Then she leaned forward and spoke so quietly that the children had to strain towards her to listen. 'I'll bet you all know Insy Winsy Spider. Shall we try it all together?'

She watched as little fingers twirled up into the air and shimmered down again in imitation of rain, and listened to her own voice echo clearly off the classroom walls. One or two of the children finally began mouthing the words of the nursery rhyme, Aida sensing the brave flutter of uncertainty in their hearts. And all the while Julian shone as clearly as the sun in summer, his blue eyes wide open, his manner so deliberate that Aida knew she had fallen in love.

Life eventually took on a reassuring pattern: school from the early morning until the afternoon, then a walk in the park before heading home to dinner in the kitchen of her furnished flat. She spent weekends with her sisters and parents, each of them somehow misplaced in the new lives they had made in a new country. When they talked among themselves about home it was always in terms of the past. Whenever Aida attempted to remind them of their sadness, they would brush her protestations aside.

'Our lives,' Sara or Mother would say to her again and again, 'cannot be postponed just because we had to leave Lebanon.'

Aida eventually discovered that despite her love for the family, it was only when she was with the children that she felt any kind of connection to her surroundings. At school, constantly wiping noses or patting the bright heads that leaned against her for comfort, or even while tying an endless number of shoelaces before a morning expedition to the garden, she could invent a world in miniature and revisit the childhood she had been forced to abandon.

Saturdays were freedom and hardship rolled into one. Aida tried not to show too much enthusiasm whenever her sisters came up with new adventures, hoping that her reluctance to join in would disguise the panic she really felt. Running in a large field behind the building she and her family lived in, she could feel herself hurtling towards certain adventure. But then she would suddenly stop, aware of the unevenness of the way, the pebbles and prickly bushes that littered the path, and of the throbbing in her feet.

Until the day Amou Mohammed accompanied the girls

to the field, held Aida's hand in his own and began a slow count to three. 'One,' he called into the wind. Aida's heart took a leap. 'Two.' She felt his grasp tighten round her own. 'Threeeeeeee,' they shouted together.

And then they began to run, Amou Mohammed pulling her behind him, their arms straining against each other; their faces turned upwards, spirits flying.

Julian treated the friends who seemed always to be around him with gracious detachment. Taking on one activity after another with the same studied concentration, he moved around the open classroom in an intimate dance that managed to display self-assurance and vulnerability at the same time.

The only preference he showed among his classmates was for Kokie, a delicate little girl who rarely spoke, preferring to sit in a corner, her dark head bent over an open book, her small body closed in on itself. Julian approached Kokie one day and sat next to her, looking into her book and saying nothing. Aida watched as the little girl ignored him and continued to turn the pages of the book with the same regularity as before. Moments later, Julian got up to join the other children.

This silent exchange was repeated several days running until Aida felt she could stand it no longer. 'Kokie, let's have a look at your book.' Aida placed herself between the two children early one morning. 'Why don't we read it together?'

Kokie looked up at Aida with a startled expression and

handed her the book without comment. Suddenly, Julian stood up and walked away.

'Well, we'll just have to do it without him,' Aida said, listening to the sound of glass breaking inside her ears.

Aida was crouched uncomfortably between a wall and Amou Mohammed's bed in his room in the basement of the building. She had sneaked in moments before and was trying to make herself go completely still so that she would not be heard. Amou Mohammed walked in, placed his prayer mat in the centre of the room and knelt down. Aida watched as he repeated the names of Allah, then bent all the way forward, placing his palms flat on the floor, before straightening up again, all the while murmuring the opening prayer with his soft voice. After bowing down several times, Amou Mohammed turned his head first right then left and then passed his hands over his face in a cleansing gesture. When he finally got up, he put on his slippers and walked out of the room without looking back. Aida stood up and wondered why he hadn't turned the light off before he left. Then she twirled round on the prayer rug and let herself out.

'You knew I was there all along, didn't you?' Aida asked Amou Mohammed on a windy winter day as he walked her to work.

'Yes, I did.'

'Why didn't you say anything?'

Amou Mohammed's rubber slippers made a shuffling

sound on the pavement as he walked. 'It was your secret and I didn't want to invade it.'

When Aida walked into her classroom to prepare for the children's arrival, she picked up a picture book and two cushions, and placed them side by side in a corner.

As she got older, it seemed to Aida that Beirut was also growing up with her. She saw what she had not noticed before: indolent young men standing on street corners, the swing of a woman's hips as she sauntered on the pavement and a certain loneliness in her own eyes whenever she looked in the mirror. Life and the city acquired hidden layers of intensity mixed with shame, so that a part of Aida could not help loving the Beirut that revelled in its own garish splendour.

She entered the International School at fifteen. Sara, who was now at university, and Dina, who remained at their old school, were gradually pushed to the periphery of her world. There were new friends and new pastimes, and a possibility of romance that filled her with dread and made her wish she had been prettier and more accomplished.

Amou Mohammed was the only anomaly in her adolescent existence, giving her a warm feeling in her heart that also made her want to leave him behind. When she asked him to help her find solutions to her own problems, he seemed too preoccupied to come up with the right answers. 'You're right, Aida,' he said to her one day as they sat in the kitchen talking, 'your mother does seem a bit troubled these days.' Then he got up to heat some water on the stove and suggested they make Mother a cup of coffee.

Sara and Dina did not share Aida's doubts about Amou Mohammed, preferring instead to behave as though nothing in him had changed, as though he had successfully stepped into their now complex and grown-up world. But Aida did not dare tell her sisters that she had glimpsed weakness in him, seen him waver between gentleness and frailty, and wanted only to turn away.

School was not much of a challenge. When teachers remembered Aida it was for being the brilliant Sara's younger sister or for her quiet patience in otherwise noisy classrooms. Aida did not mind the anonymity, realizing that it was what she had longed for all along, living inside her imagined secrets, the stories that forever tossed and turned in her head. She read as voraciously as ever when she was at home, buying books during her regular expeditions to the bookshop or raiding the crowded shelves in her mother's library. She especially loved the big hardback editions of classics and would sit in bed holding them open on her knees just as she did when she was a child. 'Goodness, that's heavy reading for you, isn't it, Aida, sweetheart?' Mother asked once as Aida sat absorbed in a very thick Russian novel. 'Are you really enjoying it?'

Aida decided to brave Hamra Street on her own. Determined to ignore the anxiety that had settled itself into the pit of her stomach, she set off early on a Saturday morning. She had put on a new pair of red jeans and a slim-fitting T-shirt, and felt both pleased and repelled by the looks of the young men she passed on the street.

By the time she reached the bookshop Aida's confidence had begun to surface and she felt a shiver of satisfaction when the salesman greeted her by name. She headed for the fiction section to browse through the shelves and settled on two novels that she'd read about in one of her mother's magazines.

When she finally came out with her purchases, Hamra Street was buzzing with activity. Aida stepped into the hub of sudden colour and confusion, and felt every bit as alive as everyone else around her. She looked into shop windows, boutiques that offered the latest fashions to elegant women in stiletto heels, and walked past street vendors who sold everything from kaak, a dry bread flavoured with sesame seeds and thyme, to roasted African peanuts in cones of newspaper. And all the while, as cars hooted their horns in rhythm and pedestrians dodged the traffic with expertise, as movement shifted into sound and then melted into pictures, Aida stored a wealth of impressions and felt her spirits soar because of them.

Moments later, she found herself walking past the Horseshoe Café where scores of young people filled tables both inside and out. They drank bitter coffee, smoked foreign cigarettes and spoke in a lively mixture of Arabic and French. Aida had heard that the café was the favorite meeting place of the students, artists and intellectuals who congregated in Beirut from all parts of the region. She imagined herself boldly going to a table, sitting down and ordering something to drink. Perhaps one of these exciting people would talk to her and she would become part of their circle. Instead, she walked slowly past the café, turning back again for one last look at what might be her future in a resplendent Beirut.

Aida began to make her way home at midday, eager to talk about the details of her morning, when she noticed a shoeshine boy sitting on a small straw stool on the pavement. A box filled with polish and brushes was in front of him and his head rested on his knees with his arms wrapped round them. His trousers were threadbare and he wore a pair of dirty thongs on his feet. As she moved closer to him, Aida realized that the boy was sobbing, his shoulders heaving under the weight of his head. She stopped to look at him more closely. Suddenly he lifted his head and looked straight at her. His thick hair fell over his forehead and although his face was streaked with tears and dirt Aida could still see the glow of light-brown skin beneath it. She was not sure how to interpret the look he was giving her but there was a mixture of concern and dismissal in her own heart. They stared at each other for a moment until the boy finally wiped a sleeve over his nose and bent his head down again.

Aida would never know why she decided to walk past the crying child that day. Once home, she found out that her mother had gone out so she ran to Sara's room and told her older sister about the boy.

'Didn't you ask him what was the matter?' Sara asked, lying on her bed with a book in her hand.

Aida shook her head.

Sara got up and put on her shoes. 'I'm going to find Amou Mohammed,' she said, rushing out of the room with Aida in tow.

Downstairs, Amou Mohammed asked Aida exactly where she had seen the shoeshine boy and told the girls he would go to look for him.

Sara insisted on coming along and turned to Aida. 'You go up home and wait for Mother,' she said, pointing her finger at her sister.

Aida watched Amou Mohammed's tall elegance and Sara's small body alongside his, both tense with purpose, as they walked away from her.

They returned an hour later as the rest of the family sat down to lunch.

'There's no sign of him anywhere,' Sara told them, shaking her head. 'We walked up and down the street he was on and then checked the rest of the neighborhood.'

Mother got up and put an arm round her eldest daughter. 'You did what you could, sweetheart,' she said. 'I'm sure he'll be all right. Now go and wash your hands and come to lunch. Mohammed, you come and eat too.'

Later that afternoon Aida went to see Amou Mohammed in his room. He was on the bed, writing on a large yellow pad. 'What are you writing?'

He looked up at her. 'It's a letter to my cousin in

Kuwait. You know, the one I told you about who works on a construction site.'

Aida nodded and Amou Mohammed continued with his writing.

She walked over to his bedside table and touched the Koran that always lay there. 'I wish I could read it like you do.'

Amou Mohammed said nothing.

'Does it tell you what you need to know?' She wanted him to say something.

Amou Mohammed put down the pad and pen, swung his feet off the bed and placed them on the floor beside her. He looked at her. For a moment Aida thought she saw the same bewilderment in his eyes that she had seen in those of the shoeshine boy. She was afraid she might suddenly begin to cry. 'We haven't done any sweeping together for a long time, have we?' Amou Mohammed said, getting up and putting on his slippers. 'Do you want to come outside and help me?'

They were standing on the edge of a large pond in a city park. It was a sunny day and the two watched as an old woman and a small child in a pushchair threw morsels of bread to the ducks and geese that floated towards them.

'That shoeshine boy has been on my conscience ever since,' Aida confessed.

Amou Mohammed was humming a tune under his breath.

'You're not listening to me,' Aida continued.

'What do you want me to say?'

She wanted him to be angry with her, to tell her that she had been wrong to neglect the weeping boy. She wanted him to say there was a way to make it up to him and to her family, and to tell her that although she had a kind heart, she did not yet know it.

'The boy got over his sadness, Aida.'

'Yes, but I didn't. I just want to know if I'm ever going to get over it.'

Whenever it came her way, love seemed always to be too late and Aida would have to readjust to its unfamiliar rhythms, pretending at passion, racing against time. The men she met were alternately kind and pitiless, generous or selfish of spirit, princes and paupers, and in all their faces she saw a version of herself that she could not recognize. 'He does not deserve you,' her sisters would tell her at the end of every romance. 'You'll find the right one soon, Aida. He'll come along when you least expect it.'

She dragged behind her a string of failures, some more spectacular than others, of artists and musicians, businessmen and academics, whose weaknesses repelled her because they matched her own. And as Aida waited for a higher inspiration, the alignment of planets, she believed somewhere in her deepest being that love, like an errant child finally come home, would eventually find her.

The photographer held a camera with a large round flashlight in one hand and a bear puppet in the other as he prepared to photograph the children for their Christmas concert. 'Hi, I'm Peter,' he introduced himself to Aida. He grinned, held up the puppet and waved at her. 'This should keep 'em happy for a while,' he said.

She rushed around with the two mothers who had come to help, pulling up trousers and straightening hair ribbons. Just before the children were due to step up onto the small stage that had been set up in the classroom, Aida called to them, 'Sing with all your hearts, children, and remember to smile.'

After everyone else had left, Peter walked up to Aida again. 'You know, I noticed you didn't do much smiling yourself.'

She looked at him. He was tall, had straight black hair and round dark eyes very much like her own. Her heart lurched.

'Hey, don't be so angry,' he continued. 'I was just wondering why you seemed so nervous.'

'You're American, aren't you?'

He nodded, then put down his camera and began to help her stack up the chairs against the wall. 'What about you? With those looks, you must come from some exotic place somewhere.'

She shrugged and didn't answer.

'Did I say something wrong?' There was a note of regret in his voice.

Aida felt as though her body were being pulled towards him. She straightened up and shook her head. 'Do you want to go out for a drink once we're done here?' she asked.

'Alone again?' Amou Mohammed asked her as she queued at the post office one morning.

'I'm always alone,' Aida snapped at him, looking hurriedly around to see if anyone had heard her.

'How long did this man last?' Amou Mohammed persisted.

She moved forward and whispered under her breath at him, 'I'm not answering your questions. Just go away.'

She saw him smile and nod at the person behind her. They said nothing more until they had stepped out onto the pavement. Crowds of people rushed past them. An old woman across the way stood staring into the throng, overfull plastic bags at her feet.

'I'm sorry,' Aida said.

Amou Mohammed shook his head. 'Let's go and help her,' he said, pointing at the old woman.

Aida ignored his remark. 'I'm lonely here.' She gestured towards her surroundings. 'Maybe I should just find some other country to live in.' She was intrigued at the thought of unfamiliar surroundings.

'Will you take me with you there?' Amou Mohammed asked before Aida walked away.

Mark arrived at the International School during the middle of the school year. He came from England, was tall and slim and wore round, wire-rimmed glasses. He had an air of stillness about him that made him seem removed from the rest of the students in the class.

Aida, now sixteen, watched him with close attention, the way he spoke and laughed, and sensed in him an inclination for tenderness.

When their English Literature teacher decided to hold a class poetry reading, Aida and Mark were among the half-dozen students chosen to participate. 'You will read two poems of your own choice and tell us why you decided to choose them,' said the teacher. 'We'll hold the reading tomorrow afternoon so you'd better meet at lunchtime to discuss the details.'

Aida arrived home that afternoon, rushed to her bedroom and began to pull books off the shelves beside her bed.

'What are you doing?' Dina asked as she came into the room.

'Looking for poems.'

Dina flopped down on her bed. 'What for?'

'It's for school, Dina,' Aida replied impatiently. 'Now, will you let me concentrate?'

It took hours for her to make her final choice. After dinner she returned to her room and read the poems out loud again and again, until she felt she had nearly perfected the rhythm and intonation of each.

At school the next day Aida's excitement was so great that she felt as though she had a big secret inside her. As they walked into the classroom, she found herself smiling at Mark for the first time.

During their lunch hour the six students assigned to read poems met in the cafeteria. Mark pulled out a chair for Aida and sat down next to her. She took out the sandwich her mother had packed for her that morning and pretended to eat.

'Why don't we begin by deciding what order we should go in?' Mark began.

Once that was decided, they told one another what poems they had chosen to read.

Aida discovered that Mark had picked the same Robert Frost poem she had. 'I was going to read that,' she told him, showing him the poem marked in her book.

'Oh, that's one of my favourites,' he said.

She tried to hide her disappointment.

'But it's all right,' Mark continued. 'I have time to find another poem. You go ahead and stick to the two you've already chosen.'

They began to spend most of their free time at school together after that, talking of everything they could think of and marveling at their likeness to one another. And when Mark took her out to a café after school one day and put his arm round her shoulders, Aida felt an instant recognition of human closeness.

It was late at night and Aida sat on her living-room sofa leafing through a book of American poetry. The Frost poem lay on the page like a memento from a happiness long past. She ran her fingers over the typescript and whispered the cadence in the poet's words.

'Whatever happened to that young boy you liked so much?' Amou Mohammed was sitting in the armchair opposite.

Aida jumped. He had never visited her at the flat before. 'Whom did I like so much?'

'You brought him to meet me once,' Amou Mohammed replied. 'He had a foreign name.'

'Mark.'

Amou Mohammed nodded as though he really recognized the name. 'He told me he hoped to become a writer some day,' he said.

Aida wrapped her arms round herself. 'I don't know what happened to him,' she continued. 'I never heard from him after the war broke out. His family must have left as well.' She closed her book and looked at Amou Mohammed. She almost felt like offering him something to drink.

'He was a good friend, then?' he asked.

'It was as though we had grown up together, you know? Sometimes I felt as if he was my brother and not just a kind of boyfriend.'

They both smiled shyly.

'He was the kind of man that I could have stayed with for ever.' Aida paused. 'If it hadn't been for the war.'

She longed for the sun most of all, the certainty of its existence, splendour and gold caressing her skin. In the watery sunlight of European cities, Aida imagined herself on beaches, in water, walking through the shimmering heat, the sky above dusty balconies small but open and her nose sniffing out the oily smells of summer in Beirut. And everywhere she went, when the novelty of uncharted places and her own inclinations bumped into each other, there was a hint of home burning under the sun.

The last year of the war in Lebanon was madness multiplied tenfold. They heard of anti-aircraft rockets being fired between neighbourhoods, of people being dragged from their homes and dumped into mass graves half alive, of militias turned into protection mafias and of an absence of mercy in people's hearts. It was to be the country's last and most terrible descent into violence before the end of the civil war.

A few weeks before his death, Amou Mohammed sent Aida a letter telling her of his hopes for the future. 'The politicians have finally met and have drawn up conditions for a ceasefire,' he wrote. 'We are all confident that the fighting will be over soon and I am praying that you will then be prepared to return, that you will take this opportunity to come back to the only home you'll ever have.' He told her he now had the courage to walk through parts of the city that he had not visited since the war began. 'I think of my walks now as expeditions because all the neighbourhoods we once knew have changed a great deal,' wrote Amou Mohammed.

There is much destruction, Aida, and a suffocating melancholy that has descended over the areas haunted only by militias and invading armies over the last fifteen years.

But despite the ugliness, there are glimpses of beauty. Only yesterday, I was walking past the American University and saw a beautiful gardenia growing by a barricade. It had been placed on top of a sand barrel and had barbed wire round it for protection. Even these wretched fighters still have some humanity in them.

He had taken to appearing in the armchair in her living room, never staying long but leaving her with an anxiety that he might call to her in sleep or stray into her dreaming. She preferred their encounters in leafy parks or half-empty pavement cafés where she could fail to notice him long enough to gather a measure of composure. Once or twice she saw him enter her classroom and sit among the children as they worked. 'You cannot interrupt me at school like that, Amou Mohammed,' she told him crossly one night as they sat in the flat. 'It distracts me from my work.'

'I like to watch the children you care about so much.'

He did not come to school after that, choosing instead to meet her at the gate and walk her home whenever the fancy took him.

It was raining very hard and she'd had a very difficult day at school. When Amou Mohammed appeared under her umbrella and took her arm as she walked, Aida felt irritation creep over her. She pursed her lips and determined not to say anything. He did not seem to mind the silence. 'What is there to hum about?' she finally asked him.

'I'm happy,' replied Amou Mohammed, 'but I gather you aren't. What's the matter?'

'What do you think?' She stopped and sighed. 'I feel so sad most of the time. It's as if the darkness will never leave me. I miss the light from home.'

The rain dripped down the edges of her umbrella and made puddles at their feet. When Aida looked down, Amou Mohammed's bare toes had turned blue with the cold. They began walking again.

'It rains back home too,' said Amou Mohammed.

'I know. But for some reason I only remember the sunlight.'

When they finally reached her building, he removed his arm from hers and stepped back into the rain.

Later that evening, as Aida sat reading his last letter to her, Amou Mohammed returned.

'You were so wrong about those fighters.' She looked up at him. 'I can't believe you had something good to say about them.'

He wandered around the room, fingering the piles of books lying untidily on the shelves.

'They tended flowers during the day and murdered people at night,' she continued. 'Isn't that what one of them did to you?'

A pained expression crossed his face. 'He was just a boy, you know.' Amou Mohammed spoke very quietly. 'Probably more afraid than I was.'

Aida suddenly felt suffocated by the calm that had descended over the room. 'How could you forgive him?' she asked angrily. 'How could you do that to me?'

Aida and Sara were having lunch in the cafeteria of the hospital where Sara worked.

'They work you too hard here,' Aida told her sister.

'Most of the time I really love what I'm doing. I don't mind the long hours.' Sara's small face lit up as she spoke. Aida thought she had the most beautiful eyes of all, almond-shaped and shadowed in different tones of her own olive skin.

'How are things going at the school?' Sara asked.

'Fine, but things seem to have settled into a routine.'

'That's what work is all about, Aida.'

'I just thought it would be different working with children.'

The two women turned to their food and began to eat.

Moments later, Sara looked up and Aida felt she could almost see her sister thinking, the wheels of her sharp brain turning in deliberation. 'Well, maybe you need to do something else,' Sara finally said.

'Like what?'

'I'm not sure, but I do know that you've never been happy here.'

'Where can I go?'

Sara let out a loud sigh and reached for her sister's hand. 'I decided a long time ago that I was not going to put my life on hold while waiting for the war to end back home,' she told Aida. 'I studied, got married and got a good job, and now I have a beautiful son. I'm very happy with my life, but I'll tell you one thing, Lebanon's the only place where I have ever really felt the earth beneath my feet.'

It was a Friday afternoon and Amou Mohammed came to pick up the sisters to take them for a walk on the Corniche. He arrived at their doorstep dressed in a long-sleeved shirt and his dark hair was slicked back and shiny. When they got downstairs, Amou Mohammed took Dina's and Aida's hands, and asked Sara to lead the way. 'We'll go up to the Raouche rock first and then walk down to the amusement park,' he told them.

Aida skipped beside Amou Mohammed and listened to her younger sister chattering away. Sara walked ahead, turning back every now and then to look at them and smile. Once on the main road, Amou Mohammed called to Sara and they crossed over to the other side together. Dina joined Sara at the railing to look out to sea.

Aida tugged at Amou Mohammed's hand. 'Can we go and look at the rock with them?'

He nodded and led her to where her sisters were standing. The Raouche rock stood, large and imposing, in the water close to the shore. It was shaped in a kind of arch at the very bottom through which small boats could go to get to the other side.

'What's all the green stuff on the outside?' Dina asked.

'It's seaweed and algae,' Sara replied. 'They grow on the rock's surface.'

Aida felt a sudden pleasure at her sister's cleverness and pulled down on Amou Mohammed's hand once again.

'Yes, sweetheart, yes, *habibti*?' he said, looking down at her.

She wanted to tell him about the huge happiness that welled inside her, like the sheet of blue water that spread before them and seemed endless. 'Can we get some corn on the cob?' she asked instead.

Burly men pushed barrows filled with all kinds of treats along the length of the Corniche. There were hot African peanuts and boiled fava beans flavored with lemon and sprinkled with salt. One man carried a large brass pot filled with bitter Arabic coffee over his shoulder and clicked a rhythm with the small china cups he carried in his hand. Another rode a bicycle that had a wide tray fitted to its handlebars, which was covered with rich Arabic sweets that stuck to the roof of the mouth and smelled of flower water. The girls and Amou Mohammed approached a barrow where a man waved a large piece of cardboard back and forth over ears of corn that were cooking over a coal fire.

'I want mine black on the outside,' Dina said.

'Well cooked, you mean,' Aida told her.

Her younger sister ignored the remark and continued to jump up and down beside the barrow. Sara reached into her pocket and took out the money Mother had given her.

Aida watched as Amou Mohammed placed his hand over Sara's and returned it to her pocket. 'No, Sara,' he said, shaking his head.

'OK, Amou Mohammed,' Sara said. 'Thank you.'

'But Mother said you must make sure to pay for everything,' Aida told her sister.

The man took one ear of corn off the fire, wrapped it in a piece of paper and sprinkled it with salt, moving in smooth, practiced motion. Then he handed it to Amou Mohammed.

'This is for you, Dina.' Amou Mohammed smiled and gave it to their younger sister. 'Is it black enough for you?'

Aida tugged at Sara's arm. 'Mother said he can't afford this, Sara,' she said in a low voice. 'Do something.'

'Just thank him and be quiet, Aida,' Sara said, shrugging off her sister's arm and taking her piece of corn from Amou Mohammed.

They ate sitting on one of the stone benches that lined the Corniche. Amou Mohammed crossed his legs and Aida noticed for the first time that he wasn't in his rubber slippers but had on a pair of black loafers that had been recently polished.

'Oh, look, Amou Mohammed is wearing Daddy's shoes,' Dina blurted out.

Aida felt her face go red with shame. She looked at her younger sister and frowned.

'They are nice shoes, aren't they?' Amou Mohammed said, patting Dina on the back. 'Your mother gave them to me only yesterday. I thought I'd wear them for our special day.'

Aida jumped up and ran to the railing. The sea looked

suddenly flat and unmoving. She felt gentle hands on her shoulders.

'Do you know what my daughter Huda says to me when I go to the camp to visit the family?' Amou Mohammed asked her. Aida shook her head and Amou Mohammed bent down to whisper in her ear, 'My love for you is as wide as the sky, and as plentiful as the sea and all its waves.'

Aida was kneeling down to help Julian on with his jacket at the end of the school day.

'I won't be coming back here next term,' he said quietly.

She finished doing up the buttons on the jacket and patted him gently on the chest.

'Are you going to a different school, then?' she asked, trying to smile.

Julian shook his head. 'We're going to Australia.'

'That'll be very exciting, won't it?'

He moved closer to her and put a hand on her shoulder. They looked into each other's eyes for a moment.

'I shall miss you, Julian.'

He nodded. 'They have koalas in Australia, Miss Aida.'

She put her head back and laughed out loud. 'Yes, they do, Julian. They most certainly do.'

Aida informed the school that she would not be returning the following term and began to prepare for her trip. She went for a brief walk in the park on the eve of her departure.

'You'll miss the trees most, I think,' Amou Mohammed told her as they made their way to the pond.

Aida smiled. 'You're right.'

The park was looking particularly beautiful: damp and green and empty.

'Things have changed there, you know,' said Amou Mohammed. There was a note of warning in his voice.

'I know, I know. But I'll love it anyway.'

He said nothing and motioned to a bench by the pond. They sat down and watched the flat expanse of water roll gently towards them.

'You told me once that poverty meant having to surrender one's life entirely into God's hands every moment of the day,' said Aida. 'Do you remember saying that?'

He shook his head. 'I said so many things in those days.' His voice appeared to be folding into itself so that she could hardly hear him.

'You're not taking it all back now, are you?' she asked, leaning closer towards him.

Amou Mohammed shifted in his seat and gestured at the water. 'It's so peaceful here,' he said. 'You can almost feel yourself melt into the background, just like the air.'

Aida was suddenly confused. 'I don't understand,' she told him. 'I thought you wanted me to go back.' She clenched her fists together and tried to calm her heartbeat. When she looked at him his head was in his hands and his shoulders were heaving. 'Amou Mohammed, Amou Mohammed, what's the matter?' She forgot her own anxiety and reached out to touch him.

He slowly lifted his face to look at her. Tears sparkled between his eyelashes. She withdrew her hand. 'I'm tired, Aida.'

The pond floated on itself and the trees stood perfectly still. Behind her, Aida heard the click, click of footsteps on the path. She took a deep breath. 'If I go back, you won't visit me any more, will you?'

Amou Mohammed did not reply and Aida felt totally alone. 'I don't know how to say goodbye, either,' she said to the emptiness beside her.

There was an uncharacteristic quiet in the arrivals hall of Beirut International Airport. Aida collected her baggage and went through customs. As she made her way through the main terminal she realized that the only people around besides the passengers were soldiers and airport personnel. Where were the crowds that usually swarmed in the airport, she wondered.

She pushed her trolley towards the automatic doors at the front of the terminal and stepped outside. A huge crowd of people shifted restlessly behind metal barricades at the entrance to the airport just ahead of her. Those at the front were facing the entrance, scrutinizing arriving passengers and waving their arms in greeting, while hundreds of others milled about in the background, talking and walking around from one end of the concourse to the other or trying to push their way to the front. The noise coming from the crowd was deafening. In the semi-darkness of sunset, Aida felt she was watching one large wave of unceasing movement. She took a deep breath and walked towards the throng of people in search of a taxi.

Hours later Aida had showered and eaten, and was standing on the balcony of the fifth-floor apartment she had grown up in. The shabby streets the taxi had driven through on the way from the airport had shocked her. Once elegant areas with luxuriant trees and wide, clean streets had become bare and dusty. There were soldiers and barricades everywhere, and an insistent air of gloom that filled Aida's mind with doubt. But looking out at the view now, at the sea and flickering lights before her, she thought she had a sense of the old Beirut and of its perfumed air.

The directions she had been given led Aida to a neighbourhood in the southern suburbs of Beirut. She had discovered that Amou Mohammed's family had a flat in an old four-story building adjacent to the refugee camp. Um Hisham and two of her children were there for the summer and Aida had called to tell them she was coming to visit. She made her way up the stairs to the third floor. One or two front doors had been left open so that Aida could see into over-furnished living rooms where men and women sat together, smoking nargilehs and talking. They looked at Aida and greeted her as she passed.

Huda opened the door at Aida's knock. Of all Amou Mohammed's children, she looked most like him: the same high cheekbones and round eyes outlined by unusually straight lashes. Aida stepped in and hugged the young woman. Um Hisham stood in the background, stouter than Aida remembered.

Aida felt tears welling in her eyes as she held on to Um Hisham.

'Welcome, Aida. *Ahlan, Ahlan,*' the older woman repeated. 'Come in.' She led Aida to a good-sized living room furnished in pale-green velvet. 'Come in and sit down.'

There was a very large picture of Amou Mohammed hanging high on one wall of the room. It was a retouched photo of an unsmiling young man who was looking away from the photographer and into the distance. Framed passages from the Koran were placed on either side of the photograph. The calligraphy was beautifully ornate, the words flowing into one another to create a single image.

'How is the family, Aida?' Um Hisham was asking her. 'How are your parents and sisters?'

'They're all very well, thank you. We have been so concerned about you . . .' Aida faltered and realized that she had started to cry. Huda got up and handed her a box of tissues and although Aida wiped her eyes thoroughly, the tears would not stop. 'I'm sorry,' she muttered through the tissue. 'I'm so sorry.'

No one said anything for a while after that. When Aida finally looked up, Um Hisham was still sitting in the armchair opposite. Huda was nowhere to be seen. 'It's just seeing you again, Um Hisham. It brings back the memories.'

'I know.'

'How many of the children are here with you?'

'Only Huda and Ahmad,' Um Hisham replied. 'Do you remember Ahmad? He's getting married next week.'

'*Mabrouk*. Congratulations. What's he doing now?'

Um Hisham began to tell her about the family, what each of them was doing and how many grandchildren she now had. Eventually, Huda walked in with coffee and cakes, and the three women ate and drank as they exchanged news.

Aida was confused. She had come thinking she would talk about Amou Mohammed and her memories of him but Um Hisham kept steering the conversation in different directions so that Aida was forced to follow.

Finally, the older woman excused herself and left Aida and Huda sitting on the sofa. There was an awkward silence that was finally broken by Huda. 'My mother doesn't like to talk about him any more, you know.'

'I understand,' said Aida, not understanding at all. Her eyes moved to the photograph and lingered there for a moment.

'Are you happy?' Huda asked.

Aida shook her head, partly in surprise and partly in reply to the question.

'My father always hoped that you would all return once

the war was over,' Huda continued. 'He talked about you and your sisters often.'

'He was very special to us. Like a second father.'

'Dina and Sara are married now, aren't they?'

Aida nodded.

'When my father heard that they had married foreigners, he felt sure they would never come back here to live,' Huda said.

Huda put one hand to her breast and smiled at Aida. Her fingers were long and tapered, just like Amou Mohammed's had been. 'Years ago, when Beirut was under siege and there was heavy bombardment, we used to go down to the basement of your building for shelter.' When their home, like many others in the refugee camp, was destroyed during the fighting, Amou Mohammed and his family took refuge in the apartment by the sea. Aida and her sisters telephoned them as often as they could to find out how everyone was doing. Often the sound of gunfire and bombardment reverberated in the background of their conversations.

'I remember once we were sitting in the shelter and my father was holding my little sister Sara in his lap because she was very frightened. I sat close to him and held on to his arm for comfort. We couldn't sleep because of the noise.' Huda leaned forward and looked into Aida's eyes. 'At some point during the night he turned to me and said he was glad that you and your sisters weren't there and that he didn't have to worry about you as well. He never stopped thinking about you.'

Aida covered her face with her hands. Moments later, she felt Huda moving up on the sofa to hold her close.

The apartment had grown shabby, its rooms possessing a deserted air that Aida could not fill. She walked up and down the corridor a hundred times a day, slept in a different bed each night and serenaded the moon from open windows, and still could not breathe life into her former home. When it became clear that her own presence would not be enough, Aida began to imagine her sisters, young and energetic, calling her downstairs to play, or her mother sitting quietly in the room next door, certain but invisible company.

And try as she might, she could not conjure her earlier visions of Amou Mohammed; his spirit had slipped from her and into the sea breezes that swept through Beirut. She looked for him on the steps of the building when she went out each morning and again when she returned at night. She sought their old neighbourhood haunts and watched for him to come round the next corner as she walked. And in every encounter with her past, wherever there were people and emotions, Aida waited to recover her knight in armor, her life's champion.

When she had been back a few weeks, Aida decided to search for work. It was midsummer and she wanted to make sure she would have a position by the beginning of the next academic year. She visited several schools around Ras Beirut and met with their principals, but their facilities for children fell short of her expectations. She longed for the expanse of her former classroom, for the pint-sized tables and chairs, for the many tools the children had used to teach themselves and the sense of freedom that permeated the atmosphere. When she realized that she was beginning to contemplate the prospect of a future without teaching, Aida gave up her search and decided to wait a little longer before she made a final decision.

The evening she met the doctor, Aida had spent the day at a local beach and was feeling refreshed and happy. Her skin glowed and in her manner was a hint of boldness that visited her only rarely. Afterwards, she thought the doctor must first have believed her to be someone very different from her usual self.

She was invited to dinner at the home of old friends of her parents and had gone only to replenish her store of memories of her family's life in Beirut. Once greeted by her hosts, Aida walked into the living room and noticed a middle-aged man sitting apart from the other guests. When they were eventually introduced, she discovered his name was Kameel and that he was a general practitioner at the American University Hospital. She fetched a cold drink, sat down next to him and began to make conversation. 'Tell me about yourself,' Aida said.

Kameel seemed momentarily taken aback by her remark but eventually began to talk to her about his work. He had dark eyes and the delicate features one would expect to see in a woman, and a voice so soft that Aida had to lean forward to hear it. She watched his face become increasingly animated, his hands, small and fine, accompanying his words.

'And what do you do?' Kameel finally asked her.

'I'm a nursery school teacher.'

'Ah, yes.'

They paused.

'There's a real need for educators here, you know,' continued Kameel. 'The war has been very disruptive of children's lives.'

She nodded and smiled at him.

'It's especially bad in remote areas like the village I come from where there has been no official authority to supervise schools.'

Aida frowned slightly. 'I had been thinking of taking a teaching job here in Beirut,' she said. 'But I'm not so sure I want to do that any more.'

He reached for the drink he had placed on the coffee table before him and began to sip it.

Aida felt a stirring of interest in this rather reserved man. 'Do you have children of your own?' she asked.

Kameel shook his head.

When they stood up to go in to dinner, Aida noted with satisfaction that he was only slightly taller than she so that, in her own eyes at least, their closeness seemed a foregone conclusion.

Aida and Kameel went out on a regular basis after their first meeting. He would finish his work at the hospital and come to pick her up in the early evening. They talked over coffees and dinners and sometimes into the early morning. They ate together and watched the sea rolling beneath the moon, and were equally comfortable in companionable silence.

He told her that he came from a small village in Mount Lebanon and had shown such promise at school that his parents had decided they would get him into university no matter what the sacrifice. When, at eighteen, Kameel finally made it to Beirut, he felt ready to conquer the world. He studied hard, living on the small allowance his parents were able to give him, and did so well that he gained a scholarship to study overseas. During the several years he spent at an American university, Kameel realized that in many ways the small town he lived in resembled his village back home, a refuge from the follies of urban life. 'They were the happiest years of my life,' Kameel told her over a drink one night. 'I felt a freedom that I've not been able to find here.'

'So why did you come back?'

They sat, their heads leaning against a wall, their eyes blinking in the too bright lights of a bar not far from where Aida lived. She had been watching Kameel's face grow increasingly flushed with drink and thought he might be preparing to make a major confession.

Kameel shook his head and laughed. 'I woke up one day and realized I was thirty-eight years old and in danger of cutting myself off completely from my roots. That was eight years ago.'

'But there was a war here,' Aida replied with

frustration. 'There was no real future for someone like you. What were you thinking of when you decided to come back?'

He looked at her just as her children had once done at school, with a mixture of bravery and pleading. 'I think I was looking for the one thing that everyone is looking for in this world.'

The emptiness of the room seemed to widen round them so that they could have been anywhere at all, suspended, their words echoing across ages. Aida heard herself sigh and hung her head so that he could not see her eyes. Please don't say it, she wanted to shout at him. She held her breath instead.

'Let's get another drink,' Kameel said after a pause.

They spent the rest of the evening at the bar, alternately talking and lapsing into long silences. When Kameel dropped her off in front of her building, Aida suddenly felt overcome by sadness for them both. She reached out and placed a hand on his cheek. 'Thank you,' she whispered.

Then she got out of the car and ran up the stairs.

Days followed one another, taking Aida with them, layering pictures of this different Beirut, one against the other in her mind, until she realized that she and the city were feeding off one another and hoping for renewal. Aida thought of visiting Um Hisham again and did not; she planned to find a school that would employ her and did not; and though she told herself again and again that she could learn to love Kameel, she knew she would not.

When her sisters phoned to ask how she was, Aida told them only of the sea and the heat, and of Beirut's incessant smells and noises, things they knew and for which they longed. Once she had put down the phone, she allowed herself to succumb to her fears.

One evening Aida asked Kameel why they had never gone out together in the daytime.

'Well, you know I go up to the village every weekend,' he replied.

'Why can't I go with you there one day?'

'There's no reason why you shouldn't but I spend most of the time working there and you might get bored.'

'It's the volunteer work you told me about, isn't it?'

He nodded. 'I spend Saturdays at the village health centre and on Sundays people come to see me at home. Not everyone can afford to come to Beirut for their doctoring.'

Aida felt slightly ashamed. 'I'd still like to go with you, Kameel.'

Aida and Kameel left for the village one early morning in September. The car climbed up a steep mountain road that twisted round itself and dipped into low valleys where red-roofed stone houses huddled against each other. Aida breathed in the fresh scent of pine and felt the beginnings of excitement ripple through her empty stomach. Kameel had told her that breakfast was being prepared for them at the home of one of his patients in the village so she had not eaten since the night before.

'They will wonder who I am,' she told him.

'We'll just tell them that you're a friend of mine from Beirut,' Kameel said.

An hour later they arrived at the village square. Shops stood on either side of the street and a scattering of people milled about on the pavement. Low concrete buildings stood next to old stone houses. Kameel turned a corner and drove into a gravel driveway. 'This is our first stop,' he said, getting out of the car. 'I treated Um Nizar a couple of months ago at the health center and she's been wanting me to come over ever since.' He led Aida round the side of a tired-looking bungalow where a woman sat on the ground baking mountain bread. They stopped to watch her flatten a lump of dough on a wooden stool and then deftly flip it back and forth over her forearms until it had stretched into a large flat circle. The woman then placed the dough on a quilted cloth pad and flipped it onto a metal dome that had a wood fire underneath it. Behind her was an uneven slab of concrete and a low table covered with plates of olives, tomatoes, cucumbers and a variety of cheeses. Aida turned to smile at Kameel.

'*Ahlan, Ahlan.*' A man came out of the house and extended his hand to Kameel.

Kameel shook hands and introduced Aida, then he bent down to greet the woman. 'I've brought you a friend of mine from Beirut,' he told his hostess. 'She wanted to see how traditional mountain bread is baked.'

The woman smiled at them both. 'She is welcome,' she

said. 'Please sit down, everything is ready.' Then she called out to her husband. 'Abou Nizar, bring the coffee out for our guests. I'll join you all in a moment.'

They ate the excellent food and chatted with Um Nizar and her husband, both of whom treated Kameel with a deference that surprised Aida. Um Nizar plied him with food and her husband kept patting him on the back and thanking him for the visit. Aida watched her friend settle into this new role with an almost unobtrusive dignity.

'What do you think, Aida?' Kameel asked her, gesturing at the food.

'Everything seems to taste so much better here,' she said, tearing off a piece of mountain bread and dipping it into a bowl of yogurt.

The others laughed.

'You city people don't know the taste of your own mouths,' Abou Nizar chided her. 'You should come up here more often and we'll show you what real food is.'

Aida smiled at him, feeling a sudden affection for these strangers and the man she was discovering in Kameel.

When they had said their goodbyes and got back into the car, Kameel turned to Aida. 'We'll go to the health centre next,' he said. 'You'll come with me?'

'I'd love to.'

The center was a short drive away. They stepped into a waiting room already filled with people, some of whom stood up to greet the doctor and ask after his health. Kameel shook hands with them, introduced Aida to the nurse who ran the clinic and disappeared into another room.

'I'll wait for you here,' Aida called out after him as she sat down.

The room was spacious and sunny. Kameel's patients sat on the straight-backed chairs that lined its walls, mostly in silence, some heaving a sigh or two as they shifted in their seats. Aida noticed an old woman looking intently at her. She was wearing a long white veil that covered her head and was wrapped tightly across her nose and mouth. The woman was dressed entirely in flowing black. Aida smiled but could not tell the other woman's response behind the veil.

'Are you his wife?'

Aida realized that the woman was addressing her and that everyone else in the room was waiting for her reply. 'No, no,' Aida repeated. 'I'm a friend from Beirut.'

'A doctor too?' The woman jerked her head towards the examining room.

'No.'

The woman sniffed and immediately seemed to lose interest. Aida settled into waiting just as the first patient was called in.

An hour later, Kameel called Aida into his office. 'I'm sorry but it looks like I'm going to have to be here much longer than I thought,' he told her.

'Well, why don't I go and explore the village while you're working? I'd love to take a good look around.'

'Are you sure?'

Aida nodded. 'Even if I do get lost, I'm sure people will be able to direct me back here.'

She stepped out of the clinic and into the sun, and followed the road up the hill. The valley on one side of the road was thick with umbrella pines. Aida walked by the rocky mountain face and the prickly bushes that grew out of it. Except for one or two cars that sped past her, she was completely alone. She walked, her arms swinging, her feet crushing the dirt and pebbles underneath, and became aware of the sound of crickets. The road eventually veered to the right, towards the village main street. Aida turned left onto an unpaved road that led her further up and away from the center of the town. When she began to feel the heat, the sun beating down on her head and shoulders, she decided to find some shade to rest in.

She found herself standing in the dusty courtyard of an old stone house. It had a red-brick roof and four pointed arches that lined the edges of its porch. The front door, windows and shutters were painted a rich green, as was the balustrade, which was rusty in places. Aida moved closer and stepped up onto the porch. She knocked on the door and waited. The tiles beneath her feet were mostly uneven and covered in dry pine needles. A battered old sofa stood at the farthest end of the porch beneath a thick, twisted vine. When no one came to the door, Aida went and sat on the sofa, looking out at the view. Beyond the balustrade were the village and the valley she had just seen, and still further there were more mountains. She felt an instant sense of calm and looked around to see if Amou Mohammed was nearby. What would he think of this lovely place? Sighing, Aida sank deeper into her seat and rested her head against the back of the sofa.

When she got back to the health centre some time later, the waiting room was empty. Kameel came out to meet her and asked how her walk had been.

'I've discovered the most amazing house. Let's go there now, I want to show it to you.'

They left the clinic and drove up to see the house.

'Isn't it beautiful? It looks so old and abandoned,' she said, getting out of the car.

Kameel followed her onto the porch. 'It belongs to a woman from the village,' he said.

'Is she living here now?'

'No, she left a few months ago. Packed up her things and went down to Beirut to her husband and daughter.'

Aida reached out to touch the vine and felt a tingling in her fingers. 'You mean she was here alone, without her family? I wonder why.'

'It's a long story, but I was told she finally decided to join them after many years away.'

'I wish we could go inside.'

Kameel looked at her and shrugged. 'The local midwife has the key. She was a friend of hers.'

There was a hint of impatience in Kameel's voice. Aida was not sure whether it was directed at her or at the owner of the house. 'You don't seem too fond of her,' she told him.

He turned and walked towards the car. 'I treated her many years ago while she was pregnant,' he said. 'She wasn't very friendly, that's all.'

Aida came up to him and patted his arm. He opened the car door for her. 'Let's go. My mother has lunch waiting for us.'

Back in the city, Aida continued to think of the house in the mountains. She imagined walking through its front door, wandering through spacious, light-filled rooms and feeling once again the peace that she had found there. Beirut had suddenly lost its charm, seemed tired and indifferent to her passions. She determined to go back to the village once again and spoke to Kameel when she saw him some time later. 'Do you think I could go up with you this weekend? I want to visit the house again and try to get inside this time.'

They were having dinner in a small café by the hospital. Kameel chewed his food with the same deliberation that he did everything else. Aida looked at the top of his head as he bent over his plate and waited for his reply.

'Why would you want to do that?' he said finally.

'Well, I'm not sure whether or not to tell you this because it's still just an idea, but don't you think that house would be the perfect place for a nursery school? I could almost see the children in that courtyard when I was there.'

Kameel looked at her, his lips a thin line in his tired face. 'What makes you think they would let you have the house?'

'I don't know. I . . . It's just an idea.'

Kameel put down his knife and fork and leaned towards her over the table. 'I took you up to my village to show you my work there and introduce you to my people,' he said quietly. He shook his head and sat back in his chair. His frustration seemed so focused that Aida thought she could feel it creeping onto her skin. 'It's always like this. People like you return, not having known the terrible years of the war, and you want to teach us about life.'

Aida laid both her hands on the table as she spoke. 'I didn't know you felt that way,' she said.

'You have never tried to know what I feel, Aida.'

'Why are you so angry?' she asked him. 'What have I done?'

Kameel motioned to the waiter for the bill and got up. 'It really doesn't matter any more.' She could not read the expression on his face. 'I have to get back to work. If you want to go up to the village I can arrange for a car to take you.'

Aida shook her head. 'Will we see each other again?' she asked.

'I have to go, Aida.'

She watched him walk away through the café doors, surprised at the relief she felt.

It was early evening and the seaside Corniche was quiet except for a few people who strolled listlessly past Aida as she walked. When she reached the Raouche rock, Aida stood at the railing to look out at the sea. The sky and the water were a very pale blue and the sun was setting behind a haze of cloud. A large cargo ship inched its way over the horizon just beyond the huge rock.

Aida thought she heard an echo of voices behind her, three little girls chatting as they skipped on the pavement. 'Where are you now?' she asked out loud. Then she looked round to make sure no one had heard her. When she turned her head to gaze at the water once again, she thought she felt a tap on her shoulder. She held her breath and waited for someone to whisper in her ear.

Aida tiptoed into her mother's room and sat at the ornate dressing table in front of the bed. Brushes, combs and perfume bottles covered its surface and were reflected in the large mirror on the wall above it. Opening the four small drawers on either side of the dressing table one by one, Aida breathed in the smell of the powders and creams that her mother applied to her face every morning. She pulled out a stick of lipstick, opened it and turned the cap all the way. She touched the lipstick with the tip of her finger and stared at the deep red stain it made before putting it away. An ornate bottle filled with her mother's favourite French perfume stood in the centre of the dressing table. It had a rich, musky fragrance that always lingered in Aida's nostrils long after she'd given up holding her mother close to her heart. She tipped the bottle onto her wrist and dabbed the perfume behind her ears and into the hollow in her neck.

'Aida, have you finished brushing your hair yet?' Mother called out.

She grabbed a large, soft-bristled brush and began to smooth her long hair back into a tight ponytail. She looked into the mirror and squinted at the face that stared back. Then she leaned forward until her lips were almost touching the cold glass. 'I remember you,' she whispered. 'I remember you.'

I lie alone in my unmade bed. I have pulled down the blinds and wait in the semi-darkness. It is early afternoon and I stare into the ceiling, the flatness of it, the absence of comfort and undulation. Outside are the hidden pictures of the city of our past. Amou Mohammed, Amou Mohammed, I have looked for you in the uncertain stance of lithe young men, the mark of prophets, and listened for you in the whispered exchanges of lovers. I have outlined the contours of your face with my own and written your story between the lines of the dreams of this vast world.

Tomorrow I will pack my bags and hope to run away again and find you in that place where my soul's secrets remain, somewhere from which there is no further to go, somewhere home.

PART III

PART III

If I lie perfectly quiet and gaze at the eucalyptus tree that trembles outside my window, holding my breath just a little, I can make time stand still so that even the air stops to listen to my heartbeat; then everywhere about me, through the dustless corridors of this sad place, emptiness abounds and I am young again, Salwa, the apple of my father's eye, the creator of dreams.

Look closely, Father. I am smiling and fearful no longer. I am everything that you wished for me, beautiful and light and full of hope, and in the far corners of my mind are all the stories I will tell when next we meet.

The first time I see Adnan, a brown felt hat on his large head, I am standing in the school playground watching the younger girls run aimlessly past one another, as children will. He is of average height, stocky and sturdy of foot. His face is wide and shows signs of age, a kind of absence of smoothness, and his ears, half hidden beneath the brim of his hat, are fleshy. Although he seems very nearly the right age, a distinguished-looking man some-where in his forties, I know he cannot be my father. I turn away and go back to my listless gazing.

Moments later a teacher approaches me. She places a hand round my waist and points to the man in the hat.

Then she leans down slightly so that her mouth is close to my ear. 'He wants to marry you, Salwa,' she says. 'Will you marry that man?'

I am fifteen and live with my mother and younger sister, Mathilde, in a coastal village two hundred metres above the Mediterranean. It is soon after the end of the Great War and like many people here we are poor enough to have known hunger.

Mathilde and I go to the local school because Father insists on our education, but I only pretend at learning. Although everyone tells me that I read and write Arabic very well for a girl, my heart is elsewhere, in the rainforests of South America where my father lives, a thousand days away from home.

I look carefully at the man once again and shrug my shoulders.

'He's come a long, long way to see you,' the teacher continues. She is gently pushing me towards him and I am leaning back heavily against her arm, trying not to move forward.

'From Brazil?'

She laughs and shakes her head. 'Even further away than that.'

Since I know there is no place further, I disengage myself from her grasp and retrace my steps to join the other children. 'Tell him to go away,' I call back to her.

For the past year now my mother has spoken of marriage with a certainty that makes me uneasy. I try to brush her remarks aside but she is persistent.

'We'll find you a good, Druze man who will give you the kind of life you deserve, my sweet one,' she says as she squats over the washing that she has placed in a big container in the front garden. She rubs pieces of cloth against each other again and again with her soapy red hands. I watch the water splash over the edge of the container and onto the dirt around her feet. She pushes her veil back off her face with her forearm and turns back to the washing. 'A pretty girl like you won't have to go through what I have, Salwa. God willing we will find you a good husband. Inshallah.'

I am small and thin but have felt the beginnings of roundness in my hips and thighs. My mother is especially proud of my fair hair, white skin and hazel eyes, all of which she tells me I inherited from my father. I am unlike Mathilde in that way. She takes after our mother who is tall and dark-skinned, and has large brown eyes that shine whenever she smiles.

When Mathilde and I get home from school, the man is perched on my father's armchair in the sitting room. He holds his hat on his lap and I can see that he is bald and even older than I'd first thought. He is speaking softly to my mother but stops when he sees me standing in the doorway.

'Come in, Salwa.' My mother smiles at me. 'Come and meet our guest.'

I turn round, grab my sister's hand and run with her, out of the gate and into the street.

'Where are we going?' she shouts at me but I will not let her go.

We scamper down the stone steps that lead to the village square, past the water fountain and beyond the mayor's house. When I look back, Mathilde's eyes are wide open and her hair is flying behind her so that she looks slightly wild. I stop abruptly and her body bumps hard against mine.

'Are you crazy?' Mathilde asks. Her hands reach for her hair and she moans, 'I've lost my ribbon. What will Mama say?'

I stand next to her and look round to see if anyone has noticed us. Then I reach into my pocket and take out a small piece of string that I found in the playground earlier in the day. 'Here, you can use this,' I tell Mathilde and give her the string.

She takes it and attempts to smooth her hair into a ponytail. 'We'll have to go back home eventually,' she says.

My sister is only thirteen but she is far cleverer than I am. I have not told her about the incident at school today but I can tell she is beginning to put two and two together. 'Who was that man with Mama, anyway?' Mathilde asks casually.

'I don't know but I didn't like the look of him, did you?'

She shrugs her shoulders. Her hair is now neatly tied back and she looks almost sophisticated because her head is held so high. I wait for her to say something else. 'Let's wait by the water fountain,' she says.

We sit on a nearby ledge and watch as women come to fill their clay urns. Several have small, round cushions placed on the tops of their heads to sit the urns on once they're full. The women look stiff as they walk away with the weight on their heads, their arms swinging wide to each side of them to maintain balance.

'Just how do they do that?' Mathilde asks. 'Wouldn't you get a headache carrying something that heavy on your head?'

I wonder when she will broach the subject of the man again. 'Maybe they're used to it,' I say. 'Do you suppose their brains eventually get squashed flat into the bottom of their skulls?'

We laugh out loud and Mathilde nudges my arm. I look at her, at the tattered navy school pinafore she wears and her skinny ankles sticking out from underneath, and realize she is beautiful.

'He's come to ask for your hand, hasn't he?'

Her question sobers me and I don't look at her when I speak. 'I suppose so, but I'm not going to marry him.'

'Mama says you'll have to some day. I mean we both will eventually.'

'Mother knows very well that she cannot marry us off without Father's consent.'

I stand up and begin to walk back towards the steps.

Moments later, I hear Mathilde running to catch up with me. 'Baba has been gone five years now, Salwa, and we haven't had word from him since he left.'

'That's not true,' I protest. 'We had that letter he wrote from the ship.'

Mathilde comes up in front of me and stops. She shakes her head and seems puzzled at something. 'Salwa, why can't you . . .'

I turn away and begin to take the steps two at a time. 'You'll never catch me,' I shout back at my sister and breathe hard as she chases me all the way home.

It has grown dark outside. I can no longer see the tree outside my window and my eyelids feel heavy. I reach a hand to my face and rub my eyes to will them awake. My fingers are stiff and do not bend easily.

'Mrs B?' A woman walks into the room and up to the bed. 'Are you ready for your tea now?'

She is speaking to me, I know, but I pretend not to understand.

'You haven't had anything to eat since breakfast,' the woman continues. 'You must be hungry.'

I shake my head and feign tiredness. I feel her smooth back my hair with gentle hands.

She is speaking softly now. 'Well, I suppose we can tell the doctor when he comes to see you tomorrow that your appetite hasn't been too good lately. Just push the button if you need anything, all right?' I hear her walk out into the corridor.

As soon as the cold begins, Mathilde and I sleep on a mattress next to the stove in the winter room. At bedtime, we rush to grab the spot nearest the fire and then fight to keep it through the night. Because she is bigger and stronger than I am, Mathilde usually wins in the struggle, but she sometimes surprises me by giving up just before I am ready to admit defeat. 'It's too easy,' she says, flipping her long ponytail back over her shoulder. 'You're no challenge at all. Too sweet for your own good.'

I throw a pillow at her and we screech and giggle until our mother comes to shush us into bed. 'Girls, girls. What would the neighbors say?'

When Father was here our daily lives had a formality about them. There was so much that had to be kept from him, the more mundane details of our existence taken care of during his absence, our ears straining for the sound of his return to a house that is gleaming and fragrant. Once inside, he would sit back in his chair, take a deep breath and then frown when my mother brought in the tray of food that she had prepared for him. 'Girls,' Father would call out. 'Come and sit with me while I eat.'

And Mathilde and I would approach him shyly, waiting for that moment when he felt content enough to smile and tell us about his day working in the city.

'Will you take us there someday, Father? To see the city with you?' I ask him, images of wide streets busy with people and a sense of urgency that I had never encountered racing through my mind.

'What do you want to go to the city for? It's no place for little girls.'

But I know I will eventually manage to extract a

promise from him to visit Beirut, that it will not remain so great a mystery to me.

We are more relaxed now that Father is no longer here, but his absence has brought a hint of defeat to our movements. I have noticed a faltering in our mother's step, her head bowing low when she greets relatives from the village, her shoulders folding in on themselves as she walks away.

It is light and I can hear someone moving about in the room. There is nothing for it but to open my eyes.

'Good morning, Mrs B. How about a quick bath before Doctor comes to see you?'

The thought of water on my tired, crusty skin is appealing. I look at the nurse. She is so young and pretty that I feel compelled to smile at her.

'The water is nice and warm, just the way you like it.' She removes my nightdress and passes the soapy sponge over my face and bare chest. Then she places her hand beneath my breasts and rubs gently. 'We'd better put some powder under there,' she says. 'It looks like you've developed a rash because the skin hasn't been kept dry.'

The sun taps on the window and noises hover outside the room but I follow the sometimes wet and sometimes chafing sounds the nurse makes as she works. I raise my eyes and examine the contours of her face. The kindness around her eyes cannot hide the pity I know she feels. I want to tell her that it doesn't matter, that I have long left this ancient body behind, but know she would be shocked at my indifference.

'You are a sweet lady, aren't you?' the nurse says as she dresses me. Then she surprises me with a quick kiss on my forehead before she leaves the room. The sweet scent of powder fills my nostrils and the young woman's kiss stays with me for a moment so that I can imagine the mark it has made, the stardust her lips have left behind.

My mother surprises me with a new dress. It is made of a soft pink material that clings loosely to the outlines of my body and is trimmed with a delicate white lace round the cuffs and the collar. I twirl round in it and show off my growing curves to Mother and Mathilde as they sit in the living room.

'What's the occasion?' Mathilde asks.

'Does there have to be an occasion?' Mother replies. 'She hasn't had anything new in ages.'

'But where did you get it from, Mama?' I ask her. 'How can we possibly afford it? It's so beautiful.' I am smiling until I see the look on Mathilde's face. It takes me a moment to realize what she has already figured out. I turn to face our mother. 'He bought it, didn't he? That old man in the hat!' I motion to Mathilde to come and help me take the dress off.

'He is not old and it was very kind of him to get it for you.'

'Well, he can take it right back to wherever he got it from. I'm not wearing it!'

Mother shakes her head at me and Mathilde takes the dress from me and places it on the sofa, giving it a gentle pat.

Mother crochets for our living. Hats, gloves, sweaters, dresses, shawls and blankets are scattered around our living room like abandoned lives. Mathilde and I help her put her creations together after school. On Sundays, as the sun begins to tip into the sea, our heads are still bent over colored garments, our hands still busy and industrious. Our customers are mostly from the village, women and the children who shuffle in reluctantly behind them when they come to place their orders. They sit in our living room, sipping the bitter coffee Mathilde has made and reach out to touch the balls of wool my mother displays before them.

The beautiful stranger comes through the front gate just as Mother is placing our supper tray on the floor in the sitting room. She is slim and delicate-looking, and wears a dark-green jacket that tapers in at the waist over a long straight skirt in the same fabric. She is not wearing a veil.

Mother stands up quickly and rushes to meet the woman at the doorstep. 'Come in, please. Welcome, welcome. Girls, take the tray into the kitchen and make some coffee for our guest.'

In the kitchen, Mathilde mutters to herself as she prepares to make the coffee.

'What's the matter?' I ask her.

She places the pot on the stove, fills it with water and stirs in heaped teaspoons of finely ground coffee.

'You didn't measure the water,' I protest but she does not rise to my bait. 'She's very pretty, isn't she?' I continue.

'Elegant, not pretty, Salwa.'

I shrug my shoulders. 'Anyway, she looks very rich. Maybe she'll make a big order and that will make Mama happy.'

Mathilde pours coffee into the small cups I have placed on a tray. 'You take this in,' she says as she hands me the tray. 'I'm going to have my supper in here.'

When I enter the sitting room, Mother is laying out crochet samples for the woman to look at. I hand each of them a cup of coffee and sit down. The woman smiles at me. Her skin is white and her nose and mouth are small and fine as a doll's. 'Ah, this must be Salwa,' she says. 'You are a sweet girl, aren't you?'

I notice that my mother has stopped taking samples out of the bag she keeps them in. She readjusts her veil and addresses our guest. 'You're not here to place an order?' she asks.

'Yes, yes, of course I am.' The woman seems slightly flustered. 'Let me see everything you have and then we can talk.'

She is there for a long time, examining the samples and nodding at my mother's explanations. Eventually, she settles on a bed cover in shades of cream and peach, and Mother tells her that it will take at least eight weeks to complete.

'That's fine. Winter is a few months away yet.'

Then she asks me to come and sit by her. I am afraid that she will hear the rumbling in my stomach; I take a deep breath as she puts her arm round me. 'I know someone who admires you very much, young Salwa. Do you know who I'm talking about?'

I shake my head and look at Mother but she is busy putting the crochet work away.

'He fell in love as soon as he saw you, you know,' the woman continues. 'Surely you remember?'

An image of the man in the hat comes into my mind. The woman moves in her seat so she can look me straight in the eye. 'He has come all the way from Australia. Do you know where that is?'

'Are you related to Mr Adnan?' my mother asks our guest.

'He is my first cousin.'

I feel the conversation drift away from me as the two women continue to talk. I get up and join Mathilde in the kitchen. She is scooping rice and artichoke stew into a large piece of flat bread.

'Mathilde, you can't eat all that in one go.'

She pushes the food into her mouth and grins at me. Her cheeks are stretched into two round balloons as she chews. I lunge at her and feel my heart burst with laughter.

'How are you doing today, Mum?' the doctor asks me. 'The nurses tell me you haven't been eating.' He is not wearing a white coat like all the others in this place and I am not sure he knows what he's talking about.

'Are you the doctor?' I whisper. I am using my voice for the first time in days and it is hoarse and scratchy.

'Of course I am. Now tell me what's the matter. We can't have you not eating like this.'

Richard is grey-haired and handsome, and has the blue eyes of his father. I feel the warmth of his hands on my shoulders through the nightdress. They are good, strong hands and I can see their every detail in my mind's eye. 'I want to sleep, *habibi*,' I tell my son.

He shakes his head. 'You know you can't speak Arabic here, Mum. No one will understand you. Now why don't you have a bit of this egg before we give you your tablets?'

We eat olives and cheese and dried thyme soaked in olive oil for breakfast. There are large flat loaves of mountain bread that mother places on the floor beside us and cups of hot tea to warm our hands with. Once in a while we get three eggs from neighbours who keep chickens. Mother cooks them very lightly in their shells and places them in small coffee cups, which she hands us with a smile. I carefully tap the egg with my spoon and break off the shell at its tip. Then I scoop up the soft white and yellow of the inside into the spoon and put it slowly into my mouth. It is hot and tasty, and slides down my throat with ease.

'Do they have eggs in Brazil?' I ask my mother.

'Salwa, watch out you don't drip any of that egg on your pinafore,' she says. 'And don't slurp your food.'

On our way to school Mathilde stops and grabs my arm. 'Did he like eggs?' she asks me.

'What? Hurry up or we'll be late.'

'Father. Do you remember, Salwa, if he liked eggs?'

It is a bright morning and other children are rushing past us towards the schoolhouse.

'Of course he does. He likes them soft-boiled best of all, just the way Mama makes them.'

Mathilde gives me an anxious look. I gently squeeze her arm and move away.

No one knows how improbable are my longings as I lie here waiting for you, Father. I have pictured our home in a thousand and one different ways, with you and without you, in the softness of my mother's embrace and in my sister's laughter. I have closed my eyes and seen the hills and waters of Lebanon, and remembered layers of morning sunlight shadowing me as I played. This is the telling of visions. Listen for them in your sleep, Father, and dream with me.

'It's me, Mum. I've brought you some beautiful grapes today.'

Lilly's eyes are a deep blue. She is the liveliest of my four children and always looks at me with anticipation, as though I had hidden talents that would soon come into view. 'It's such a lovely day I thought you might like to go out into the garden.'

I shake my head and watch her moving about the room with purpose. She places the grapes in a red plastic bowl, rinses them in the sink in the adjoining bathroom and brings them to me.

'They're seedless so you don't have to worry about pips.' She puts a plump yellow grape in my mouth and squeezes out the pulp. It feels squashy on my tongue and tastes sweet and tart at the same time. I close my eyes and purse my lips together and hear Lilly laugh. It is a rich sound that comes, I know, from the depths of her heart.

'Sour, is it, Mum?'

It is Sunday afternoon and Mother calls me into the sitting room to work. Mathilde is already with her, unravelling spools of white and peach-coloured wool for the beautiful lady's blanket. There is a restlessness in me and I do not feel like joining them. I sit beside Mathilde and say nothing.

'Salwa, help your sister, please.'

Mathilde looks at me and makes a face. I smack her hand and she flinches.

'Salwa,' Mother protests. 'What's the matter with you? Take some wool from the bag and set to work.'

'I don't want to marry that man, Mama.'

'And why not? He would provide for you for the rest of your life.'

'But he'll take me away from here, far away.'

Mother's eyes soften. 'He promised he would never take you away. I made him promise that.'

I shrug my shoulders. 'Anyway, I don't want to work on that woman's stupid blanket,' I mumble.

Mother shifts in her seat and looks straight at me. 'You will not be rude, Salwa.'

I remember the way the lady put her arm round my waist and held her head close to mine, the perfume in her hair floating into my nostrils. I stand up, walk out of the sitting room and out of the front gate. It takes me only a few minutes to reach the woods behind the house. I find the fig tree and climb up to the highest spot, where the thick branches have created a comfortable seat. There is an excellent view of our house from here, with the village and the blue sea beyond. I lean my head back against a branch and breathe in the sweet, sticky smell of the fig leaves. I am such a good climber that, in summer, when trees in the village are filled with fruit, our relatives come to find me for help with their picking. I heard Father once say that I was as agile as any boy but when I mentioned this to Mother later she only frowned and told me to shush.

The house looks small and sad from where I am. I imagine Mother and Mathilde, silence drifting between them, their heads bent over the crochet hooks and their hands flying. A soft spring breeze rustles through the leaves and I think I hear someone laughing. I give the tree a reassuring pat, climb down and make my way home.

Lilly is sitting on a chair by the bed. She has her glasses on and is reading. I cough quietly and she looks up at me. 'Are you all right? Do you need some water?'

'*Habibti*, did you speak to your sister like I asked you to?'

'Mum, you know I can't understand you very well when you speak Arabic. What did you say?'

'Your sister . . .'

'You mean May? She's fine, Mum. I got a letter from her last week. I read it out to you. Don't you remember?'

'No. Diana, Diana . . .'

'It's all right, Mum, dear. It's all right.' Lilly gets up and wipes the tears from my face with her hand.

On the day that Adnan and his family come to lunch I wake up early, put on the new pink dress and wrap Mother's white shawl round my shoulders. Mathilde and Mother are busy preparing food and look up at me when I walk into the kitchen.

'You look lovely, dear,' Mother says. 'I don't want you getting your clothes dirty in here, Salwa. Why don't you go inside and make sure the sitting room is nice and tidy?'

'I thought we were going to sit outside, Mama.'

'No, dear. These are special guests, remember?'

When Adnan sits next to me I feel my end of the sofa shift downwards. He begins to speak but his voice is so soft and low that I can hardly hear him.

'Adnan has something for you, Salwa,' says his beautiful cousin.

Adnan reaches into his pocket and brings out something wrapped in a large white handkerchief. Inside it are two bangles which he hands me. They are made of a rich red gold that wraps round my wrist with a satisfying clink. I have never seen anything so pretty and cannot stop smiling.

'Look at her eyes shine,' Adnan's cousin tells my mother and they both laugh.

When the guests leave, Mathilde and I sit side by side on the doorstep. It is late afternoon and as the day begins to end, the air is suddenly fresh and cool.

'That shawl makes you look very grown-up, you know,' says Mathilde.

'Mama said I could have it.'

My sister nods and begins to make patterns in the dirt with her shoe.

'You know Mama doesn't like you to do that, Mathilde. You'll spoil your shoes.' I place my hand on her knee to stop her.

'Did you like him?' I ask Mathilde after a while.

She clears her throat. 'He gave me something,' she says.

'He did?'

She reaches into the front of her dress and takes out a gold chain. It is very fine and has a charm in the shape of a bird in flight hanging on it.

'Mathilde, it's beautiful. Does Mama know?'

'She put it on me. I love it, don't you?'

I hold out my hand to show her the bangles. 'He gave me these bracelets.'

'I know. Mama said he's very generous. A real gentleman.' My sister's face is flushed and she's smiling in a way I haven't noticed before.

'His name is Adnan, Mathilde,' I finally tell her. 'Please call him by his name from now on.'

Lilly has gone. The room is bare and empty of color without her. A nurse comes in to change me. She is gentle but there is something on her mind that makes her actions seem distracted. She does not know how grateful I am for her silence, how I have longed for exactly this, the weight of age that urges me into a deep, dark stillness.

Mother wants to make the dress herself. She orders a heavy silk brocade in off-white with gold trimmings that arrives from Damascus only days before the wedding. Mathilde and I watch her as she works the beautiful cloth that folds and shimmers as she moves.

I wake up a few days later to find Mother sitting on the floor hemming the dress. She is humming quietly to herself and when she looks up her eyes are red, her eyelids heavy.

'You didn't sleep?' I ask her.

She gets up, lifting the dress with her. '*Habibti*, will you try it on now? I need to make the final changes today.'

I sit on a chair covered with garlands in the sitting room of our home, surrounded by the women of the village. It is the day of the wedding and my mother carries a large straw tray filled with raisins and walnuts, which she offers in turn to all our guests. The men and children are waiting in the courtyard for the groom to arrive. I catch a glimpse of Mathilde through the front door. She is standing by the gate with a group of girls from our school. She looks towards me for a moment and turns away again before I can catch her eye.

A woman takes the tray from my mother and whispers in her ear. Mother stands very straight with her hands on the front of her skirt. Her veil falls loosely over her shoulders and her face is uncovered. She lifts her eyes towards the sky and begins to sing. Her voice is low and slightly throaty so that the notes linger in the air after she has left them. Mama sings of mountains and the sea and lovers standing in the shade of a mulberry tree, and once she is done turns to me with a wide smile. I want to reach for her but I know I must sit absolutely still and silent as I wait.

'They're here, they're here,' someone calls out.

There is a stir of urgency among the women. My mother and sister come to stand by my chair and I feel a sudden twitch in my chest. Crowds of men come in through the front gate and form a straight line to face our relatives. With their hands on their hearts, the men greet one another, bowing their heads and repeating messages of welcome and thanks. I watch as Adnan finally makes his way past the crowd and through the front door. Mother helps me up and the women begin to ululate congratulations. Their voices are shrill and filled with a disquieting urgency.

I am holding hands with my mother and sister when Adnan walks up to us and just before I go, in that instant between home and things unfamiliar, I turn to Mathilde and give her a fierce hug and laugh at the grunt I receive in return.

I hear my mother's serenade again years later, in a small village on the eastern coast of South Australia where soft, powder-like sand reaches into the ocean and seagulls hover over giant waves. I stand at the front door of our white stone house, listening to the gramophone play the music of home. The children sleep by the warmth of the wood stove and for once, miraculously, my ducks and chickens lie quiet in their coop. And as I listen, the sounds of this sprawling country suddenly silenced, memories of that day long ago come over me, of mother's voice and the thumping rhythms of my own heart, and for that brief moment a certain joy is restored.

'I've left out all the years in between. Oh dear, oh dear. Can you help me remember?'

'Mrs B, are you all right?'

I am holding the woman's hand and pulling down on it but she will not listen. She pushes my head gently back on to the pillow and feels my forehead. 'Have you got a fever?'

'I said I need you to help me remember.'

She smiles down at me and shakes her head. 'It's all right, dear, I'll get you a pill to help you sleep. Doctor Richard will be by in the morning and you can talk to him then.'

My husband takes me with him to a house in a village across the mountains. A distant view of Beirut spreads below our bedroom window and there is a fragrant rose garden by the front terrace. My mother-in-law sleeps in the winter room by the kitchen and spends her days talking to me in a gentle, aged voice that gives me comfort.

At the end of each week, Mother and Mathilde come to see me. They are all dressed up, mother in her long black dress, a silk veil wrapped tightly round her head, and my sister in polished shoes and a shiny ribbon in her hair. I wait by the front doorstep and feel the happiness rush into my face at the first sight of them. 'Welcome, welcome,' I call out, reaching for my mother's arms. 'Mathilde, how you've grown. Just look at you, my little sister.'

Mathilde grins shyly and gives me a quick hug.

'Were the roads all right?' I turn to my mother. 'You must be tired. Come in, come in.'

The day goes by quickly. We talk, eat and sip coffee on the terrace, and all the while I think of their leaving and another night without them.

I pull Mathilde up by the sleeve of her dress. 'Come and help me in the kitchen, Mathilde.' I drag my sister behind me, leaving the two older women on the terrace.

'Stop pulling on my dress,' Mathilde protests. 'It's new.'

'Yes, I know. It looks lovely on you.' She smiles and sits on a stool by the sink.

'I thought you were going to help me with the washing up.'

'Salwa, you and I know that's not why you asked me in here. What's the matter?'

I shrug my shoulders and turn to the sink. 'It's nothing. I . . . I think I'm pregnant, that's all.'

Mathilde stands up quickly and grabs me by the arm. Her face is red and her eyes are wide open with astonishment. 'You must tell Mother.'

'I will, I will. It's just that . . .'

'What is it?'

'Have you heard anything from Father since I left?' I try to sound unconcerned.

There is a look of impatience in her eyes when she speaks. 'When are you going to stop, Salwa?'

'What do you mean?'

'I mean when are you going to stop hoping that he'll get in touch with us? He's gone and he's never coming back.'

'You sound like Mama when you talk like that.'

Mathilde grabs my hair and pulls. Then she punches me in the arm and I turn round and scream. We are locked together when Mother rushes in.

'What's going on? What's the matter with you two?'

When we finally stop and pull away from each other, Mathilde is sobbing loudly and Mother is shouting at her. 'How dare you shame me like this in front of our in-laws? How could you do this to me?'

'I think I'm going to have a baby, Mama,' I blurt out.

Mother turns to me. She takes a deep breath and tries to smile. 'Salwa, what wonderful news. May God grant you a beautiful son, my darling.' She puts her arms round me.

Behind her, Mathilde wipes her face with a hand-kerchief and though I try to catch her eye, she will not look at me.

I was born on the first day of the first month of the year. My mother says I am a New Year's baby who came into the world smiling. When my first child is born, a bright and pretty girl we will call May, I am too tired to notice the look on her tiny face, but I love her with an instant and fierce passion.

'Salwa, my darling Salwa,' Mother says as she places the baby in the crook of my arm. 'You have a beautiful little daughter.'

I remember the scent of her, her skin like silk and the expanse of her heavy-lidded brown eyes as she looks up at me. May, my beautiful one, is marked at birth with a measure of my own sadness and now it will not leave her.

'Where is she?' I call out through sleep.

'What is it, Mum? Who do you want to talk to?'

I open my eyes and stare at Lilly. She comes up to the bed, straightens the pillows behind my back and smoothes back my hair with her hands.

'May. I need to talk to her.'

'You know we can't do that, Mum. She's thousands of miles away.'

Lilly's eyes are smiling at me and my heart flutters slightly. 'Why don't we write her a letter instead?' She pulls paper and a pencil out of her handbag and sits down on a chair by the bed. 'What did you want to tell May?'

Adnan is slow and his unhurried movements have a natural gentleness. He has, I am sure, acquired this trait from his widowed mother who follows me around the house like a child grateful for company after years of solitude. She tells me news of her sons and daughters, all long gone to distant lands, and unfolds a pile of letters she keeps hidden in a burlap bag that she has placed under her mattress. 'Read them to me again, Salwa, *habibti*, will you?'

I read the letters, adding words of comfort that they have forgotten to include and pretend not to notice the tears in my mother-in-law's eyes as she sing-songs in her trembling voice, 'You see how they love their mother? You see how they think of me even when they are so far away?'

May becomes the center of our existence so that we are all kept busy from other preoccupations. We feed, wash and clothe her, and marvel at her alertness and each secretly hope that she will know a genuine happiness. Adnan holds her with his large hands away from his bulky body and looks down anxiously into her eyes.

'Don't worry about holding her, Adnan,' I tell him with a superior voice. 'She'll be fine.'

He looks up at me, shakes his head and as he hands May back to me I am almost overwhelmed with pity for him and for our distance. Ever since the baby was born he has been less forthcoming with conversation and seems concerned about something. He is himself only after he receives a letter from one of his brothers in America, though he tells me nothing of its contents. I suppress any curiosity I might have about the letter and feel reassured once again.

It is the beginning of spring and May is six months old. I dress her in a pink dress that mother has knitted for her and take her out into the garden. The air is cool but I can smell a slight change in it that makes me happy. Adnan comes out to join us and he is smiling. 'Guess where we are all going today?' he asks me.

I shake my head.

'I want you to get yourself and the baby ready. We're going down to Beirut for the day.'

I squeal with excitement and May is startled into sudden tears. 'Hush, baby. Hush now. Father is taking us to the city.'

'Hurry up now, Salwa. Bring your coat along, it might get a bit chilly later.'

I hurry inside to get changed and as I dress I hear Adnan and his mother whispering to each other in the kitchen. She begins to sob.

'Mother, what's the matter?' I rush in to comfort her.

'Salwa, go back inside,' Adnan says. 'Give her a minute. She'll be fine.'

Just before we leave, my mother-in-law holds the baby close to her chest and sniffs quietly.

'We'll be back this evening.' I smile at the old woman. 'You can put her to sleep if you like.'

Beirut is like nothing I have ever imagined. It is flat and green, and reaches out into the sea in places, and vibrates with activity. The hired car drops us off at a huge square where dozens of other cars and carriages are parked, and hundreds of people scamper between them. I giggle nervously and gently squeeze the sleeping baby in my arms. 'We're here, May,' I whisper. 'We've finally come to the city of our dreams.'

Adnan pays the driver and then turns to me. 'Let's go to the souqs first, shall we?'

The shops are lined up, one against the other, in long corridors that stretch almost as far as the eye can see. Overhead are sheets of corrugated iron unevenly placed so that the sun filters in here and there and breaks the dimness. Shopkeepers stand behind narrow counters and shout out their wares as customers walk past and push against one another, occasionally stopping to look at the merchandise.

'Come on, Salwa, just follow me.' Adnan looks back at me as he walks. 'We'll go and see some material for you and then we'll go to the gold souq.'

I know this is a day that will stay in my mind for ever. I feel the weight of my child as she leans into me. I walk behind my husband, stopping to see and touch things of beauty. I laugh when Adnan insists that I buy whatever catches my eye. He takes the baby from me so I can hold up pieces of cloth to the light and gives her back only to reach into his pocket to pay for my purchases. When we get to the gold souq I think my heart will stop with excitement. 'Oh, Adnan. This is so wonderful.' I try on a pair of earrings that dangle from my ears in diamond shapes of dazzling gold; in the mirror the shopkeeper holds up for me I see the married woman I have become, sophisticated and clever.

We eat lunch in a small restaurant off the main square and when we are done I look at my husband and smile. 'I can't wait to tell Mama and Mathilde about our trip, Adnan,' I say with a sigh. 'But I feel quite tired after all that excitement. I suppose we'd better make our way back now.'

'We've got one more stop to make before we go home.'

'Where are we going?'

'It's a surprise,' Adnan replies. 'Come on, let's go.'

We return to the square and meet up with the driver who brought us down to Beirut earlier. He drives us closer and closer to the sea.

'Where are we, Adnan?'

'We're at the Beirut Port.'

Adnan tells the driver to stop and we get out onto a concrete dockyard where people are standing surrounded by suitcases and uniformed officials.

'Adnan, what are we doing here?'

My husband is silent. I notice that perspiration is running down his forehead. The driver lifts two cases out of the trunk and makes his way towards a huge ship in the dock. Adnan and I follow him.

'Where are we going, Adnan?' I ask. 'What is going on?'

I feel a rising panic as I watch people making their way up the gangway and onto the deck of the ship. Adnan pulls me to him. The baby nearly slips from my arms and I gasp with fear. He jerks me forward and onto the gangway but I am holding back with all my strength.

'Don't be frightened, Salwa. Everything will be all right.' My gentle husband grips my arm with surprising force. 'Give me the baby, Salwa.'

I shake my head. 'Tell me first, tell me why we're here.'

But Adnan shakes his head and reaches for the baby. I pull away and May lets out a scream. 'People are beginning to stare, Salwa.' Adnan is nearly shouting. 'Do as I say and get on the ship.'

'I'll go another day, I promise, Adnan. You know I always keep my promises. Just take us home now, please.'

I am leaning against something on the open and crowded deck. I can no longer feel the tears on my face but I know they are there because they are falling onto the baby's wrap.

Adnan is standing close by and he is looking anxiously at me. 'We're going to America, Salwa. To start a new life. You'll see, we'll be very happy there, I promise, *habibti*. I promise.'

I watch as the dock moves further and further away until the bright and brilliant beauty of Beirut is only a distant memory. Then I stand up and make my way to the railing with May in my arms. I lift my child into the singing wind, open my mouth and shout out the beloved names of my mother and sister again and again so that everyone turns to look. This time Adnan does nothing to stop me.

'Wake up, Mum. I've got a surprise for you. Wake up and have a look at this.'

When I open my eyes, I see the drifting light of another dying afternoon coming through the window. There is a vastness in this country that even the sun can recognize so that at the end of the day, when the sky folds in on itself, it does so with reluctance rather than hope. I turn my head to see Richard standing by the side of the bed. He is holding something in his hands which he lifts up to show me.

'Hello, dear,' he says with a smile. 'Look what I've brought you, Mum. It's a CD player. You can have music all day long and even at night if you like. It'll just take me a few minutes to set it up.'

My son loves me with an eagerness that sometimes has his father shaking his head with affectionate dismay. At ten years old, Richard is slim and strong, and has reddish-brown hair that blows off his high forehead when he stands in the wind. He is good and happy, and makes me think of sunny days in autumn.

'What's that?' I ask him when he comes through the front door one Sunday morning.

'It's a cornet, Mum. Mr Roberts is teaching me how to play.'

'Mr Roberts?'

'The old man who sits outside the hotel,' May says from the sofa. 'You've heard him playing that trumpet, haven't you?'

'Richard, are you telling me you've had that thing on your mouth?'

'It's OK, Mum, it's clean,' he says and then turns to his sister. 'It's not a trumpet, silly,' he tells her. 'It's a cornet.'

I lather soap on a wet cloth, take the instrument from him and wipe it all over.

'Be careful, Mum, you'll get water inside it,' Richard protests.

May giggles and tries to grab at her brother. I rub the cornet with a dry kitchen towel until it shines.

'Leave your brother alone, May. Here you are, *habibi*. You can play it now.'

Richard stands very straight, places the mouthpiece to his lips and leans his head back. When he blows into it, a terrifying sound splits the air and May lets out a loud shriek. My son turns to me with an embarrassed grin. 'I guess it'll be a while before I learn how to play properly, eh, Mum?'

The sound of waves fills the room and my racing heart is instantly calmed.

'Isn't it lovely music, Mum? Do you like it?' Richard places both his hands on my arm and looks down at me with infinite tenderness.

I try to smile.

'You'll have no trouble getting to sleep now, will you, dear?' he whispers.

You must long for a son, Father. In the steaming cities of South America, somewhere between waking and sleep, when your spirit wanders into dreams so that there is no stopping it, you think of him, I know. He is there when you look into your mind's eye and every time you venture into the man you left behind, into that moment when life held its breath and you were free to abandon me.

'We won't be staying here much longer,' Adnan tells me as we prepare for sleep in the spare room of his brother's home in a small Louisiana town.

I say nothing and continue to tuck little May in her crib by our bed. 'Sleep now, baby,' I sing to her the way my mother taught me.

'I got a letter from Adelaide this morning,' Adnan says a moment later.

'From your brother, Norman, in Australia?'

Adnan nods and seems relieved at my reply. 'He says we're to go there right away. He'll take care of everything.'

Just like your other brother said he'd do when he told us to come over here to stay with him, I say to myself.

Adnan seems tired and old tonight despite his show of cheerfulness. I walk over to him, place my hand on his shoulder and give him my best smile. 'We could always go back home, dear,' I tell him. 'We'll be well taken care of there.'

'Go and live with my old mother in a country that holds no future for our children? Is that what you want, Salwa?'

I shake my head and press my lips tightly together because the bitterness will not lift itself off my chest. My husband may not know it, but there is fire in me yet.

A week later we are bound for Australia. We stand on a railway platform waiting for the train that will take us to the American west coast where we will board ship. I hand my brother-in-law a letter. 'I forgot to post this, Najm. It's for my mother. Would you send it for me?'

He nods kindly and puts a bundle of newspapers tied with a string in my hand. 'These are from home,' Najm says. 'They're not very recent but I thought you might enjoy reading them during the trip.'

I thank him, take May from the arms of my sister-in-law and board the train.

'We are very happy to be leaving, Mama, darling,' I write her. 'Najm and his wife treated us well but there are few opportunities here and Adnan is certain things will be better in Australia. Please don't worry, Mama. We are well and May is growing more beautiful every day. On this great voyage of my life, you and Mathilde are always in my thoughts. But no matter how far my journey, I will be back to see you again, you can be certain of that.'

The train's constant movement lulls May to sleep and Adnan dozes on and off at the far end of our seat. I am by the window alternately looking out and trying to read the newspapers that my brother-in-law gave me as we were leaving. Two other passengers, a young man and his wife, sit opposite. They whisper to one another and occasionally look up to smile at me.

The newspaper in my hand is months old but I am too happy with news of home to worry about that. I turn to the second to last page of the newspaper and realize that I am looking at the obituaries. I read the names of dozens of men and women in a clear, bold print. They form loops, sharp angles and thin lines that never meet so that the words seem almost like drawings. I feel my body sway forward, against the train's movement, and hear a sudden shout: 'Are you OK, lady? You look like you're about to faint.'

The young man sitting opposite is by my side and speaking into my ear but I cannot bring myself to answer him. I feel him push my head down towards my feet and my stomach heaves. My hands open and the newspaper I am grasping so tightly falls onto the floor.

'Mister, hey, mister, wake up.' The wife is speaking now. 'It's your daughter. She's not well.'

A moment later Adnan's shoes appear next to mine. 'She'll be all right,' he says in a sleepy voice. 'Thank you for taking care of her.'

'Look, I'll fetch her a glass of water,' the young man says. 'Just hold on to her so she doesn't fall over.'

Adnan is next to me on the seat. He pats my back and asks me if I can lift my head up. Once I am sitting up, he hands me a glass of water. I sip it slowly.

'What's the matter, Salwa? What happened, dear?'

I shake my head and look out of the window at the darkening landscape. I see no houses, no trees and in the sky the moon's light is rapidly fading. I hear a rustle and look round to see Adnan pick up the newspaper. He puts on his glasses and begins to read. Then he turns and reaches for me. I lay my head on his shoulder, the scent of his sweat and tiredness filling my nostrils, and begin to weep.

'Is she all right?' The young woman's voice is soft.

'She's had some bad news,' Adnan tells her.

The train moves steadily along the track and the night closes in on the world and for just one moment my husband's voice is the only sound I hear: 'It's her father. She just found out that he's passed away.'

The nurse lifts my upper body and props me up with pillows. I have just had my bath and she wants me to look at the way she has fixed my hair. Fragile waves of silver-grey hair are brushed back off my face and forehead. My eyes look glazed over and my nose is like a small but perfect ball in the centre of my face.

'I've got some make-up for you as well,' says the young nurse. 'It'll cheer you up, Mrs B.'

When she is finished with me my face looks unfamiliar but I am amused by the result.

'See what a little make-over can do? Much nicer to receive your guests looking your best, isn't it?' the kind nurse says.

I am not sure if it is the doctor's turn to visit today. I wonder what he will think of me looking this way.

'Hello, Mum. Are you ready for your surprise?'

My son and daughter saunter into the room with big smiles. They come up on either side of the bed and I immediately feel the warmth of their bodies close to mine.

'Remember I told you someone special was coming to see you, Mum?' Richard asks; then he motions to a figure in the doorway to step inside.

The boy is tall but stocky and wears thick-rimmed glasses that cover the top half of his face. He walks up to the bed with purpose and places a hand on my arm. His touch is light on my skin. He leans over and kisses me on the cheek. '*Sittoo*, how are you?'

My face must show astonishment because Richard interrupts the child before he can continue. 'Mum, it's Nabil, May's boy. He's grown into a fine young man since we saw him last.'

I look up at my grandson's face. 'Oh dear, oh dear.' I feel flustered for a moment. 'How are you, *habibi*? The family, are they all well?'

'You see that, Nabil?' says Richard. 'She insists on speaking Arabic and you are the only one who can understand her. You'll have to translate.'

We all laugh and I reach up to touch Nabil's face. 'Your skin is like velvet, my sweetheart. Just like your mother's.'

May is the most beautiful of my daughters. She has a face as bright and clear as a new moon and dark eyes that taper into either side of her face like neat almonds. She is gentle and there is a certain quietness about her smile, in the slow, upward movement of her mouth and the sudden appearance of a dimple in one cheek that lends relief to her loveliness. By the time she is sixteen years old her admirers, young men and old, trample over our doorstep with gifts and promises that she dismisses with unwavering determination.

'I won't do what you did, Mum,' she tells me. 'I won't marry and leave home so soon.'

When, some ten years later, May finally meets the man who will become her life's partner, it is during our first journey back to Lebanon and that is where I am forced to leave her, a million miles away from home and me.

After my bath I tell the nurse that I want to be put in a wheelchair.

'Right away Mrs B. It's wonderful to see you so cheerful today. I'll get an orderly to help us, shall I?'

From the window I see my grandson arrive through the front entrance. He is wearing a light-brown wool cardigan with black buttons that lends him an air of maturity.

'You made this jumper for Dad several years ago, remember, *Sittoo*?' Nabil says, giving me a hug and kiss. 'I liked it so much I took it away from him.'

We go out into the garden. It is a sunny day and the trees and grass are an even, deep green. Nabil sits down on a bench under an enormous oak and pulls my chair next to him. 'Sure you won't be too cold out here, *Sittoo*?' he asks.

'I'm fine, *habibi*, just fine.'

I look closely at him and he shifts slightly in his seat. 'Mum sent you this.' He takes a thick envelope out of his jacket and hands it to me.

I shake my head. 'I can't open it, Nabil. My hands . . .'

'I'm sorry, *Sittoo*. I'll do it for you.' He pulls out two pages folded over a small stack of photographs. 'It's a letter, I think, and some pictures of the family.'

'I can't see without my glasses, dear. Why don't you read the letter to me?'

'All right.'

'Mum, darling,' my grandson reads. 'How lucky Nabil will be to see you. Since I cannot leave the family and make the long trip home, I thought I'd send you my gorgeous son for his school holidays. He is fifteen years old now and during his father's frequent absences from home is the man of the house. Isn't he wonderful?' Nabil stops and gives me a sheepish smile.

'Go on, *habibi*, go on.'

I think of you all the time but know that you are well taken care of, especially with Richard and Lilly by your side. We are all well here, thank God, although Riyad works too hard and we don't spend enough time together as a family. But I suppose that's the way of the world these days. I have found an old photograph of us all in Kingston from years and years ago. I must have been about eleven at the time. Don't I look cheeky standing next to Richard with that big grin on my face?

Dad looks a lot older than I remember him at the time. I know that life there must have been pretty tough for you sometimes but I have wonderful memories of my childhood and know this was mostly because of you and the happy face you always put on for us. You look your usual pretty self in this picture. Young and eager, as Uncle Jim used to say.

I think of those times often, Mum, of how happy and close we all were and feel that you have all been too far away for far too long. I wish things could have turned out differently. But whatever happens, I will come back to see you again, my darling mother. You can be certain of that.

'*Sittoo*, are you all right?'

I look up at Nabil and nod. 'I'm fine, just a little tired, that's all. I think I'd like to get back into bed now. Will you call the nurse for me?'

Mathilde and I are standing on the shore. Our feet are bare and the water is lapping over them in gentle waves. I feel myself gradually sinking into the sand and almost lose my balance. I reach out and grab my sister's shoulder and she squeals.

'You'll make me fall over, Salwa. Let go of me.'

She is seven years old but has already acquired the lean, vigorous body that she will maintain for the rest of her life. I ignore Mathilde's remark and hold on tightly. The water has already reached the hem of my dress and I feel the fabric stick round my legs. 'Look, there's a huge wave coming,' I shout with delight.

Mathilde places her hand on my shoulder and squeezes hard. We hold our breath and wait. When the wave comes it beats against our legs and pushes us backwards. I wobble and lean towards my sister, then fall onto my bottom. As Mathilde lets out a shout of triumph, I hear my mother calling out from behind us, 'Mathilde, what have you done to your sister this time?'

We are driving to Kingston; Adnan, the children and myself. It will be an all-day trip, Adnan tells me, and we must do our best to make ourselves comfortable in the old Chrysler. Diana sits in my lap in the front and the older children are in the back of the car, taking turns at the window. I am saddened at having to leave Adelaide, at saying goodbye to the friends I managed to make there during the past five years, but the depression has hit this country badly and we have no choice but to seek opportunities elsewhere.

'Norm has a shop there now, Salwa, and he wants me to work with him,' Adnan reassures me once he has made the decision for us to move. 'We'll live in the house right next door to the business. Being in the country will do us all a lot of good. You'll see, we'll be very happy there, dear.'

When we arrive in Kingston it is already early evening. The children scramble out of the car with obvious relief. The sea air is fresh and soft on our faces, and wakes us up into instant cheerfulness. Adnan's brother greets us at the door of the shop and although I know him well enough I feel a sudden nervousness when I shake his hand. He is the most stern of the six brothers and I am not sure how things will be with him living so close by.

'Welcome, Salwa,' says Norman. 'Welcome to you all.'

The children are happy. They love the smallness of the town and revel in the freedom of a steady, unhurried life. Adnan has lost the constant restlessness that once plagued him and goes about his business with undisguised satisfaction, a kind of swagger to his step. I am busy, cheerful and content with the new-found stability in our existence, the certainty of my children's love and the growing affection I have for my husband. And somewhere in the back of my mind, in that corner where joy lies hidden among memories, I am surprised at the unencumbered pleasures that fill my new life.

'Come on, Mum, eat up, this is your favourite.'

I am sitting up in bed and Lilly is urging me to taste the pudding she made for me earlier this morning, but I am reluctant to try it. 'Not too much flower water and plenty of sugar, just the way you like your mhallabiyyeh, Mum.'

I finally accept a spoonful of the pudding and am pleasantly surprised by the taste. It slides smoothly down my throat and I open my mouth for more.

Lilly looks pleased. 'See, Mum? I'm not so bad at Lebanese cooking, am I, now?'

I remember Lilly's past cooking failures, her frustration

at never getting a dish quite right, and feel laughter rising up in my throat and into my face.

'Mum? Are you laughing at me? You naughty thing.'

We both giggle uncontrollably. As I look into my daughter's face, the ease with which she laughs at herself and her vibrant, lovely eyes, a sudden happiness swells inside me.

'You've always been an insufferable giggler, haven't you?' Lilly asks me as soon as she can take a breath.

My new friends at the Country Women's Association tell me I am musical. 'You have an ear for it, Sally, and a lovely voice too. You should try to do something about your talent.'

We are at Mrs Taylor's for afternoon tea and I have brought along a round rich fruit cake that everyone is enjoying.

'Have you ever thought about taking music lessons?' Mrs Holt asks me as she sips her tea.

'I've always liked the piano, I suppose.'

'Mrs McCornick gives lessons, you know. Why don't you ask her if she'll take you on as a student?'

'We don't have a piano at home what with the children, the cooking and my husband and his brother . . . I don't know.'

But later that evening, as Adnan and I sit together in the sleep-out after the children have gone to sleep, I broach the subject with him. 'What would you think about getting a piano?' I whisper so as not to wake Richard who is fast asleep in the corner. 'The children might enjoy taking lessons and I could help them.'

'Why, do you know how to play?'

'No, but I could certainly learn. You know how much I've always liked music.'

Adnan says nothing and I know that his silence is better than an outright no.

The children and Adnan are sitting around the breakfast table and I am piling their plates with the eggs and bacon that have begun to sizzle on the stove.

'So where would you put it, then, Salwa?'

'Put what, Adnan?' I ask, and my heart is fluttering in my chest.

'The piano. Do we have room for it?'

I lean over my husband and plant a big kiss on his bald head, and smile when the children giggle with delight.

'Never got the piano . . . he never got it for me.'

'What is it, *Sittoo*?' Nabil asks from the chair in the corner. 'What did you say?'

'Oh dear, oh dear. What will become of me?'

Nabil walks up to the bed and lays a hand on my arm. 'I didn't hear what you said.'

'Adnan, he never got me the piano he promised.' I'm trying to speak as clearly as possible but the boy looks puzzled. 'Norman told him I might start getting new ideas and want to go out and perform in front of people. I never would have done that, you know. I just wanted the music, that's all. Not too much to ask, is it?'

'Do you want the nurse, *Sittoo*? Is there something hurting you? Are you asking for the nurse? What are you trying to say?'

'He and his brother, when they made up their minds about something they just wouldn't listen.' I shake my head, close my eyes and hope to drift into sleep.

'It's another boy,' Mathilde writes.

He is big and docile like his older brother, though he has my dark colouring and funny nose. The delivery was fine and I am up and about, and as strong as ever. I don't know what I would do without Mother. We have taken over her house and her life but she seems happy to have us here. And despite all the demands that Shafiq and the two boys make on my time, I still manage to free myself every Sunday afternoon to work with Mama on her crochet projects. The money comes in handy in these difficult times.

Salwa, Salwa, our times together seem so distant, like you. I imagine you have become a sophisticated Australian lady now, well travelled and with a foreign air about you. I, on the other hand, have not changed, not so that you would notice, anyway. Marriage and children seem only to have stretched out a life that was already there, already me. I miss you and hope we will be together again.

I am sending you some pistachios and a bag of cracked wheat with this letter. The sweaters are for the girls. Mother and I hope they like them. May God keep you and your family healthy and safe.

Your sister,
Mathilde.

Adnan has promised to teach me how to drive. We get into the car and drive up to the beach where he plans to give me my first lesson. We have left the children behind but when I put my head through the window and look back, I see them jogging at a leisurely pace behind us, all four of them, Diana trailing not too far behind. I try to shoo them away with my arm but they take no notice.

'What are you doing, Salwa?' Adnan asks. 'Who are you waving to?'

He starts to look in the rear-view mirror but I poke his arm to distract him. 'It's nothing. I'm just a little nervous, that's all.'

The road that runs alongside the beach is wide and, to my relief, empty of other vehicles. Adnan stops the car and motions to me to get into the driver's seat. As he makes his way round the front of the car to get in beside me, I steal a glance behind us and see the children standing still in the distance.

'The first thing you have to learn is to get the keys in the ignition and to start up the car,' Adnan says with a determined voice. 'Show me if you can do that.'

This is an easy task and I begin to gain some confidence.

'Good,' Adnan continues. 'Now let me tell you about the pedals.'

Once I have repeated the names of the levers at my feet to him several times, we move on to the next thing.

'The tricky part is coordinating the gears with the clutch, but you'll get used to it.'

Adnan's remark reassures me further and I feel I can now enjoy the lesson. I look into the rear-view mirror and attempt to raise my hand to wave at the children.

'Salwa, concentrate on what you're doing, please. This is no joke and you'll have to take it seriously if you're going to learn how to drive properly.'

I place my hand on the gear shift as Adnan instructs me to do, push down on the clutch and learn to change gears, one, two, three, reverse, one, two, three, reverse.

'Good.' Adnan nods. 'Now, let's switch the car back on and we'll try to move forward.'

The engine hums quietly around us. I push down twice on the gas pedal and look at my husband. 'It sounds good, doesn't it, *habibi*?'

'Just keep your foot on the brake, Salwa. I'm going to let go of the hand brake now.'

I feel the car loosen a little.

'OK, let's get into first gear and then you can let up on the gas pedal a little.'

When the car moves forward I squeal with delight. 'Adnan, this is great. I can drive, I can drive.' I stick one hand out of the window and wave it back and forth. 'Children, look, I'm driving.'

'Salwa, focus on what you're doing, for heaven's sake,'

says Adnan in an irritated voice. 'It's time to change gears again. Push the clutch down now.'

But in my excitement I can no longer tell which pedal is which and my feet suddenly feel heavy and unco-ordinated.

'Not the gas pedal, Salwa. Take your foot off the gas pedal!'

The car lurches forward. I lift both feet up and lean heavily onto the steering wheel. 'Oh dear, oh dear.' I jump at the sound of the car horn.

Adnan leans over and fiddles around with the ignition until the car comes to a stop. The lock of hair that he usually uses to try to cover the top of his head has flopped over one ear and his glasses are askew. He is breathing heavily and he has the look of utter frustration on his face that he gets whenever I fail to do what he wants me to. I begin to apologize but burst out laughing instead. And as my husband and I stare at each other, the children come running to the car. They open the doors and jump in.

'Are you all right?' Richard begins. 'Does Mum know how to drive yet, Dad?'

'She nearly crashed the car, didn't she, Dad?' Lilly's voice is full of wonder.

'Mum, why are you laughing?' May asks me as Diana plops her small self in my lap and begins to play with the steering wheel.

Adnan remains silent throughout this exchange. I know he is angry but I cannot stop giggling. Once the children grow quiet, he turns to them. 'Since you seem to find this situation so funny, you can all walk home.' He steps out, walks over to the driver's side of the car and motions for me to get out.

I lift Diana out and onto the ground, then take her hand and call to the others, 'Come on, children, let's go home. It's a nice day for a walk.'

Later that night, Adnan turns to me in bed. 'How about we forget about the driving lessons, Salwa?'

'I gave you a real fright, didn't I, dear?' I say to him.

Adnan reaches out to touch my face and I glimpse the beginnings of a smile on his. 'I'll survive,' he whispers.

Beyond this window and the tree that stands outside it, beyond the city that surrounds us, out where sky and earth appear to meet, this country reaches out, measureless and extraordinary, a refuge in a far-flung world.

'Good morning, Mum. How are you doing today?' Richard strides into the room and moves towards the window. 'Let's open this, shall we?' he says. 'It's a beautiful day out.'

The air that touches my face is fragrant and spring-like, and I let out a big sigh.

I hear Richard laugh out loud. 'Enjoying that fresh air, aren't you, Mum? You look wonderful today. Got make-up on?'

I shake my head and smile. 'It's nice to see you, son.'

Richard bends down and plants a kiss on my cheek. 'So you've decided to speak to me in English again. Thank goodness for that. How was your breakfast this morning?

Did they give you soft-boiled eggs like I asked them to?'

'Richard, I've been thinking,' I begin quietly.

'Hm?' He approaches the CD player and turns to me. 'How about some music? Something gentle.' A sweet strumming floats over us, the sound of string instruments and a trumpet in the distance. 'I knew you'd like this.' Richard stands by the bed and touches my face. 'We've always been music lovers you and I, haven't we, Mum, dear?'

'Listen to me, dear,' I continue with an insistence in my voice. 'I've been thinking.'

'What is it, Mum?'

'Do you remember when they took you away? Do you remember that?'

'You mean during the war? Are you talking about when I was in the army, Mum?'

I nod. 'How long were you gone for?'

'What does it matter? I came back, didn't I? It was all right in the end.'

'It seemed like for ever to me.'

'I know, dear, I know. But it's over now. Don't think about things that upset you. Doesn't do any good, Mum. Doesn't do any good to worry about what's long over.'

May is in the sitting room making up packages for the boys overseas. She fills them with rich fruit cakes, knitted woollen socks and balaclavas, bars of soap and razors, and then adds a brief note with words of encouragement and hope. I imagine those poor, lost soldiers, two or three months and thousands of miles later, tearing the packages open, running grubby hands lightly over their contents, perhaps closing their eyes for a brief and anonymous feel of home.

Ever since Richard was called away, May has thrown herself into action, showing a strength of spirit I did not know she possessed. She tells me little of her purpose but I have seen passion in her eyes and know she does this because simply waiting for the worst to happen would be impossible for her.

'Mum, Mum, there's a letter,' Diana rushes through the front door waving the letter in her hand. 'It's from Richard.'

I look at May and know we are both thinking the same thing: he is still alive, or at least he was when he wrote that letter.

'Call Lilly and your father,' I tell my youngest daughter. 'We'll read it together.'

I hand the letter to May.

She opens it and waits until Adnan and Lilly have walked in from the shop next door with my brother-in-law Norman. 'Shall I start reading now, Mum?'

I nod and motion to the men to sit down.

Dear all,

I am well and working hard. If the medical corps doesn't give me the necessary training to become a doctor then nothing else ever will! I expect I'm seeing things here that I never would have in peacetime.

There are many injuries and almost as many deaths but we are doing the best we can. The few doctors here are doing marvellous work and I am proud to be working alongside them. I miss you all more than I can say and hope that you are holding up fine in these difficult times. Mum, don't worry, I am well fed and get rest when I need it. Dad, I'm sure you and Uncle Norm are holding the fort as usual. I miss you both very much. And as for you girls, I hope you're taking care of each other and not giving Mum and Dad too much trouble. Please keep writing. Your letters and packages mean more to me than you could ever know. And don't forget to give my love to Uncle Solomon.

> Yours,
> Richard.

'Uncle Solomon?' Diana asks. 'He never writes about him.'

'Well, he thought of him this time,' Lilly tells her sister.

'He's trying to tell us something,' Diana continues in an excited voice. 'Don't you see? He's letting us know he's in the Solomon Islands. That's where our troops are stationed.'

'And in New Guinea,' says Adnan. 'I think Diana's right, Salwa. That must be why he mentioned Uncle Solomon. What do you think, Norm?'

It is early evening and I am in the kitchen preparing dinner. I hear footsteps behind me and feel a hand on my arm.

'Are you all right, Mum?' May asks me. 'Did the letter upset you very much?'

I turn to her and shake my head. 'I'll be all right, dear. Don't worry about me. Why don't you set the table for me and we'll have dinner soon.'

As soon as May leaves the kitchen, I stop what I am doing and open the back door. The ducks and chickens are fretting because I have forgotten to feed them. I step outside carrying the scraps in a large container under my arm and go into the coop. I breathe in the damp and musty smells that have become so familiar over the years and then call to my animals to come and feed. They scurry around my feet as I scatter the food, pecking and clucking with anxiety first and then satisfaction. 'Come on, babies. Come and eat, come and eat. I forgot about you, didn't I? *Yalla, yalla.*'

When next I see him, when next I hold my son in my arms, I will have a thing or two to say. I will tell him that war does not prepare you for life, that instead it tears what life there is in you away. I will say that waiting is agony, even in the uncluttered corners of this sleepy town, and that his sisters, fragile as they are, are brave and strong for me. And last of all, I will tell my son that wherever he goes in this world he will always encounter the same truth, that mothers and their children must never be made to part.

'*Sittoo, Sittoo.* Are you awake?'

The boy is standing by the bed, touching me hesitantly on the shoulder. He is leaning over me and I see the anxiety in his large dark eyes. 'I'm fine, *habibi*. Don't look so worried, I'm just fine.'

He lets out a long sigh. 'I came in and you were talking in your sleep or something.'

'I was just thinking out loud, that's all. Old people do that all the time.'

He nods and smiles. 'I got you a new CD, *Sittoo*. Uncle Richard and I found it in a shop in the city. Shall I put it on for you?'

A melancholy tune that brings love and heartbreak to mind floats around us. When the singer's voice rises high into the words of sadness that she sings, I turn to my grandson. 'Who is she?'

'Fairouz. Do you remember her, *Sittoo*? Mum said they took you to see her in concert at the Baalbek ruins when you came to visit us when I was little.'

I see lights and magnificent columns rising out of the darkness and hear music that makes everyone round me stir with recognition. 'Yes, *habibi*.'

'You like Lebanon, don't you, *Sittoo*? I mean I know this is your home now but you enjoyed going back, didn't you?'

Lilly and Diana have been sick since we boarded ship a few days ago. They toss and turn in their bunks and rush to the lavatory next to the cabin clutching their stomachs.

'I'm getting off as soon as we get to Fremantle and that's all there is to it,' Lilly says during a respite from her distress.

'So am I,' echoes Diana.

The woman we share the cabin with smiles. She is returning to England after many years away and is familiar with difficult voyages.

'This is the toughest part of the journey,' May tries to comfort her sisters. 'Once we get to the open sea, it'll be a lot smoother.'

'I don't care,' Lilly protests. 'I still want to go back home. I never wanted to go on this trip anyway.'

We are making our way to Lebanon and my three daughters will not be swayed from their lack of enthusiasm. They are afraid of what will come and I cannot blame them for there is a certain anxiety in my own heart at what I will find back home after twenty-seven years away. 'May, stay with your sisters until I get back. I'm going to find your father.'

Adnan's cabin is on the other side of the ship but I find him leaning over the railing on the deck. 'What are you doing here, dear?' I ask. 'It's too rough out.'

'I know. I just wanted to get away from the cabin for a bit.'

We stand together for a moment, looking out at the ocean.

'The girls are still unwell. May seems to be all right, though.'

'Do you think they'll like it there, Salwa? I mean enough to stay.'

My heart skips a beat. 'But what about Richard, dear? We've left him behind and he can't do without us.'

'Don't you want the girls to find good husbands? I thought that was what you wanted. You're always harping on about it.'

'But there are plenty of Druze boys back home. We don't have to go all the way to Lebanon to find them.'

'We're not going to discuss this any more, Salwa,' he says after a pause. 'Are you going to join me for lunch or not?'

I nod. 'I'll just go and get May.'

Beirut shines in the distance and I can hardly control my excitement. The coastline is jagged, and coloured in shades of green and a dusky yellow. As we get closer we can see the buildings that dot the landscape, white stone structures with slanting red roofs and the roads that run beside them. It is early spring and the sun caresses the shoreline, making vague shadows between the trees.

'Oh, Mum, it's beautiful.' Lilly lets out a sigh.

'It is, isn't it?' May says.

'I told you it was.' I laugh. 'We're home, we're finally home.'

I put a hand on Diana's shoulder and squeeze it. 'You're going to love it, girls, just you wait and see.'

I hear Adnan chuckle. 'Come on, let's get ready to go ashore,' he tells the girls. 'We don't want to keep your aunt waiting too long.'

As soon as I catch sight of Mathilde just beyond the gangway, I run to her. We hold each other close and I smell the rich, clean smell of her dark skin. She is wearing a veil but I pull it off and bury my face in her hair. It is thick and black, and done up in a plait.

'Salwa, what are you doing?' Mathilde lifts the veil back onto her head and laughs.

I put my hands round her face and smile. I have a thousand things to say but can only repeat her name: 'Mathilde, Mathilde.'

She pushes me gently away from her. 'Let me look at you. You look wonderful, Salwa, *habibti*. Just wonderful.'

I can feel my daughters and Adnan waiting behind me. 'Come and meet your aunt, girls.' I draw them to me and introduce them one by one. 'They don't speak any Arabic but they can understand a lot of what we say.'

'Salwa, they are so beautiful.' Mathilde reaches for each of them.

Adnan greets my sister and cousin Toufic who accompanied Mathilde to the port. A porter takes our baggage and we begin to make our way to the car.

'Mathilde, is that you?' A large woman walks up to us with her hand extended.

'Iqbal, how are you?' Mathilde shakes hands with the woman. 'This is my sister Salwa and her family. They're here from Australia.'

'Yes, I know. I'm meeting someone off the same ship. What beautiful young women they are.'

I feel the girls bristle at the familiarity with which she speaks to them.

'We're relatives, you know,' the woman says and when they don't respond she turns to me. 'Do they understand what I'm saying? Don't your girls know any Arabic?'

'Of course they do, they're just tired after the trip that's all.'

'Well, Salwa, now that we've met, make sure you bring them up to the mountains soon. I have a young man in mind I want them to meet.' She turns to May and gives her a big smile. 'This one is the most beautiful by far. I'm sure Riyad will like her. He's my brother-in-law. Wonderful young man, educated in America.'

I mutter a quick goodbye, nudge Adnan and we herd the girls away and towards the car.

'What was she talking about, Mum?' May asks me. 'Why did she keep looking at me?'

'Let's get home, girls,' Adnan says. 'Let's go.'

'I just have to make a quick stop on the way,' cousin Toufic says as we finally get into the car. 'It won't take long, just twenty minutes or so.'

Adnan sits in the front passenger seat and the five of us squeeze in the back. I feel suddenly anxious and want to get the girls home as soon as possible. We drive out of the port and up towards the city center. I recognize the huge square from my last visit to Beirut, but it is more crowded with cars and people than I remember it. 'Adnan, look, this is where you brought me . . .' I realize our day in the city many years ago might be one he would like to forget and cut my sentence short. Toufic turns right and into the souq area. The car makes its way past the entrance to the gold souq and into a narrow street where there are vegetable carts on either side. Men are shouting out their wares and people pack the pavement, stepping on and off when the crowding gets too much.

'I'll just stop here for a minute,' Toufic says as he gets out of the car.

'You can't leave the car in the middle of the road like this,' Adnan calls out after him, but he is already out of sight.

'Don't worry, Adnan,' says Mathilde. 'He won't be long.'

'For heaven's sake, Dad. Shut that window. It's so noisy out there,' says Diana.

She frowns and places her hand over her eyes. May is staring out of the window with a look of total astonishment on her face and Lilly is leaning her head against the back of the seat. A child comes up to the car and taps on the front window. His face is streaked with dirt and his hands smudge the glass. Somewhere behind us a car horn toots loudly.

'This is the best vegetable market in the country,' Mathilde says. 'People come from far and wide to get their produce from here. Toufic is going to get us some mouloukhiyyeh. We'll have it for lunch tomorrow.' She reaches for my hand and gives it a gentle pat. 'You don't know how wonderful it is to have you all home at last.'

Lilly moans beside me and I turn away from my sister.

'Mama was already gone when I got back,' I tell Nabil.

The music has stopped and we have been sitting in silence for some time.

'What is it, *Sittoo*?'

I shake my head at him. He reaches for a tissue and gently dabs at my eyes. 'You've always looked like your father. Handsome young man he was.'

'My parents met on your first trip back, didn't they?' Nabil asks me. 'Mama told me they were married six weeks after their first meeting.'

I pat the side of the bed and he comes to sit by me. 'It all happened quickly. She was so beautiful in the dress it made me cry just to look at her.' I stop for a moment and feel Nabil breathing quietly beside me. 'I tried to stop her,' I whisper. 'The night before the wedding, Lilly, Diana and I begged her not to go through with it but she wouldn't listen.'

'She loved my father.'

'She thought she was doing the right thing.'

'The right thing?'

'She thought it would make us, her dad and me, happy.'

Mathilde waits for the thick, dark liquid to come to the boil before she turns off the fire on the stove. The aroma is rich and fills the kitchen as she pours the coffee into two small cups.

'Those are the same cups Mama used, aren't they?'

'They came with the house, *habibti*. Come on, let's go and sit out in the courtyard.'

It is a warm, sunny day and we sit in a shady spot by the front door.

'The children are all at school?' I ask my sister.

'They all set off early this morning so we have the day to ourselves. I thought we might go and visit old Uncle Basheer later if you feel up to it.'

I nod and take a sip of my coffee. It is strong and fortifying.

The village is noisier than I remember it. Sounds of car engines are persistent and there is a feeling of constant bustle that permeates the air. It's almost as if it has acquired a sense of self-importance that it never had during my childhood. 'Is it me or has the village changed a great deal?' I ask Mathilde.

'It's been twenty-seven years, Salwa. What did you expect?'

'You're right. I just had this image in my mind . . .'

Mathilde adjusts the veil on her head, folds one arm over her stomach and with the other balances her cup on its saucer. She is still sinewy thin with long, delicate-looking legs and narrow ankles, but her shoulders have begun to droop a little.

'Do you ever hear from Shafiq?' I venture to ask her.

She crosses one leg over the other and takes a sip of her coffee. 'He's been gone three years and I've only ever received two letters from him. He sent them when he first got there. He sends a bit of money every now and then but that's all.'

'He's in Brazil, isn't he?'

She nods.

'Just like Father was.'

'He's more like Father than you know, Salwa.'

A faint breeze blows the front gate open and I stand up to shut it. 'These hinges need oiling,' I say to no one in particular. 'How do you manage with the six children and the house to take care of?' I ask Mathilde once I have sat down again.

'I get by, don't you worry about me.'

'I wish I lived closer to you. It's so difficult being so far apart.'

Mathilde puts down her coffee cup and reaches for my hand. 'It's difficult for both of us, *habibti*, but at least we're seeing each other now.'

'Adnan wants the girls to marry, but they don't like it here at all, Mathilde. They keep telling me how much they hate it and say they want to go back home.'

'Couldn't you find any suitable young men back in Australia?' she asks me.

'Do you think he and his brother let anyone near the girls? He's too strict with them, doesn't give them freedom. May wanted to be a doctor but he wouldn't hear of it.'

'That's too bad.'

'She was so smart at school too,' I continue. 'Always top of her class.'

We finish the rest of our coffee in silence.

Mathilde takes the tray into the kitchen. 'I'll just put my shoes on and we can go on those visits now,' she calls out behind her.

I stand up and walk to the edge of the courtyard and look at the small field just below us. It is planted with orange trees that are beginning to bloom and the soil is a beautiful dark-brown colour. I take a deep breath and find somewhere inside it a hint of the familiar scent of orange blossom. I fight the urge to jump down into the field to be near the trees that stand warm in the sun, and wrap my arms tightly round myself instead.

As soon as darkness falls my mind wakes up to thoughts of you, Father. I am alone and afraid, and have no claim on the night but this hard, insistent desire to understand what it was that compelled you to leave us. Did you search your memory for tenderness and then wipe it away or was it a sense of adventure that drove you to forgetfulness? Did thoughts of the family you once cherished leave you unhurriedly or was it an instant realization that overtook you?

I have children too. They are constant and firm, and love me beyond measure, and I know that when I leave them, when that sweet quiet sweeps over me at last, they will know what passions lingered in every chamber of my heart.

'Lilly, Lilly, are you there?'

'Right here, Mum.' My daughter comes up to the bed so I can see her. 'Can I get you something?'

'I think I'll have my breakfast now.'

'Just give me a minute. I'll go and get it for you.'

Lilly returns with a large tray, which she props up on the bed. On it is a plate with fried eggs and a stewed tomato.

'Where's the bacon?' I ask.

'They ran out of it this morning, Mum, but Cook told me she'd have some for you tomorrow morning.'

'Humph, the service here isn't too good, is it?'

Lilly lets out a loud guffaw.

'It's not ladylike to make that sort of noise, dear,' I tell her. 'You've always had a loud laugh.'

She dips a piece of buttered toast into the yolk of the egg and feeds it to me.

'Put some more salt on the eggs, Lilly. You know I like my eggs salty.'

Lilly shakes her head and gives me a big smile. She likes it when I'm perky like this.

'Diana liked her eggs sunny side up,' I say between bites.

'Yes, she did, didn't she?'

'I knew how she liked her food. Cooked it exactly the way she wanted it, always.'

'You certainly did, Mum. She loved your cooking.'

'Even towards the end, when she couldn't eat everything and she was in so much pain, I made sure she ate well and enjoyed her food.'

I chew slowly because my new teeth are still a bit uncomfortable. 'I miss her,' I tell Lilly.

'I know, sweetheart. I do too.'

'She's always in my thoughts, you know. Especially now when I have so much I need to think about.'

'You're keeping busy with your thoughts, aren't you?'

I stop eating and look Lilly in the eye. 'Don't you make fun of your old mother,' I say angrily.

Lilly laughs and reaches out to touch my arm. 'Mum, it's just that you looked so serious for a minute . . .'

I feel the muscles in my face relax. 'How come you can always make me smile, young lady?'

'It's because you love me so much, Mum. Now stop talking and eat your breakfast.'

Diana is small like me and like me has a round nose that makes her look for ever like a child. She is my youngest and because of that I feel bound to look out for her even as she grows older and needs me less. We live together in Adelaide in a comfortable two-bedroom bungalow we bought soon after Adnan passed away at the ripe age of eighty-two.

Of all my children, Diana is the only one who has not married and I am grateful for her company. She works at an office near the city and I take care of things at home. I watch her as she gets ready every morning, the way she lingers over her make-up at her dressing table and then looks with horror at her watch. 'I've got five minutes before the bus gets here, Mum.'

I reach for a dress from her cupboard, put it over her head and hastily do it up for her. She slips on a new pair of tights, steps into her brown shoes and rushes to the front door.

'Have a good day, Diana, dear.'

'See you this evening, Mum,' she calls out as she runs for the bus.

It is a quiet life yet there is a certain satisfaction in it, the kind that comes with old age and unexpected freedom, and I am not prepared the day my world changes for ever.

'The news is not very good, Mum.' Richard comes to see me the evening after Diana has her operation. 'She's not doing too well.'

'But I was with her this afternoon,' I protest. 'We talked and she told me she felt fine.'

Richard shakes his head and big round tears fall from his blue, blue eyes.

A nurse charges into the room and startles me when she turns the lights on. 'Time to change you, Mrs B,' she says briskly. 'Your dinner will be here soon.' She takes off the cover and proceeds to remove the diaper. She is so businesslike about it that it saves me any embarrassment. 'I'll just get a sponge to clean you up a bit, shall I?'

I nod wordlessly and succumb to her ministrations. She is almost done when I decide to speak up. 'It's not what you expect to happen,' I say slowly in English.

'Hm?'

'I mean you never think that you'll outlive your own child.'

She puts on the clean diaper, adjusts my nightgown and pulls up the covers. Then she goes to the sink and washes her hands. She turns out the light and returns to the bed, her figure illuminated round the edges by the light in the corridor. 'Your hair needs to be seen to, Mrs B,' the nurse says and I see that she is holding my hairbrush in her hands. 'Why don't I do that for you?'

The bristles of the brush are so soft that they seem to caress my scalp. I look beyond the window, at the lustrous moonlight in an immense black sky and no longer feel so small.

'I'd like to go to the village today,' I tell May as we sit drinking our coffee.

Riyad left earlier this morning and the children have just gone off to school.

'The village?'

'To the house I was born in, dear. I want to see it.'

'It's been shut up ever since Aunt Mathilde moved down to Beirut, Mum,' says May. 'I don't think we'd be able to get in, anyway.'

I stand up and take the coffee cups into the kitchen, trying to hide my disappointment. May follows me and stands by the sink. 'I can get someone to drive us up there, Mum, if that's what you really want to do.'

I have been back with May and her family for nearly two months now. It is soon after Diana's passing and I am happy to be so well surrounded. My daughter puts her arm round me and I lean my head against her shoulder.

The front gate is unlocked and groans when we push it open. I step into the courtyard. It has been cemented over and there are no flowers in the bits of earth that line its edges. The tree that once shaded the front door is no longer there and all the windows are boarded up. I walk to the end of the courtyard and see that the orange grove below has gone. In its place is a grey-concrete two-storey building. I watch a woman hang up washing on a line on the first-floor balcony.

'We should have brought Aunt Mathilde with us to let us into the house,' May says.

I turn to her. 'No, no, it's all right, dear. We don't have to go inside.'

We are facing the house and I am surprised by how insignificant and unattractive it looks. 'It's not how I remember it,' I say, shaking my head. 'Even during my last trip when Mathilde and the children were still here . . . it was different then.'

May puts her hand on my shoulder. 'Houses are like that, Mum,' she says quietly. 'They need to have people in them to stay alive.'

Richard and Nabil walk into the room. They seem tired and agitated at the same time.

'Here we are, Mum.' Richard bends down and gives me a kiss.

'Hi, *Sittoo*,' Nabil says. 'How are you today?'

My grandson's face is flushed and he is almost breathless.

'What's the matter, *habibi*? Have you been running or something?'

'He's just excited, Mum,' Richard replies. 'We went to see the local secondary school and Nabil liked it very much.'

'I might go there next term, *Sittoo*,' Nabil grabs my hand and squeezes it. 'Mother said I could stay if I wanted to.'

'Stay here? What about your family?'

A pained expression crosses the boy's face and he turns to his uncle.

'Nabil, why don't you go and get us all something cold to drink,' Richard tells him. 'Here, take this money, there's a small shop round the corner.'

As soon as Nabil walks out of the room I motion to Richard to come closer to the bed where I can see him clearly. 'Are you planning to keep the boy here?'

'It's not me, Mum. I spoke to May last week, they've been having problems with him at home. May and Riyad both feel he might do well to be away for a while.'

'What kind of trouble?'

'He's not doing too well at school and can't seem to focus on anything.'

I feel flustered and don't know what to say.

'I think his father's too tough on him at times and he feels under pressure to perform,' Richard continues. 'You know how Riyad can be at times.'

'You're going to help him abandon his home?'

'Nabil will be with us. We all love him and he's very happy being here.'

I shake my head and reach for Richard's arm. 'You mustn't let this happen, Richard, please. Promise me you won't, dear. Promise you'll send him back where he belongs.'

Nabil walks back into the room. He is carrying a large bottle of soft drink and three plastic cups. He pours out the drink and hands us each a cup.

I lie back on my pillows as soon as they leave, feeling suddenly overcome with tiredness. I used to be stronger than this. Now all I can muster around me is frustration and a sense that life has better places to go.

It is Monday morning and I am in the wash-house with Janet. We sort through the washing and then feed the fire under the copper.

'I think we can put the whites in now, Janet.'

'Yes, Mrs B.'

I stand by as Janet carefully places sheets and pillowcases into the now boiling water. She then adds the soap and stirs the wash with the long thick stick that I keep leaning against the wash-house wall. Janet has come to help me with the washing, as she does every week.

'Let's leave those boiling for a while before we rinse them, Janet. Would you like your cup of tea now, dear?'

'Yes, thanks, Mrs B.'

I go into the house and put the kettle on for our tea. I like the quiet of Monday mornings when the children are all at school and Adnan and his brother are too busy in the shop to come into the house for frequent breaks. I reach for the biscuit tin and place it on the table.

Janet comes in and sits down. Her dress is torn in places and she is wearing a pair of overlarge men's shoes on her feet. Although she is several years older than I am, I feel protective of her at times.

'How are your children, Janet?'

'All right, thanks, Mrs B.'

'They can be a handful sometimes, can't they?' I ask as I offer her the tin.

Janet nods and takes a biscuit.

'Sometimes I wish I could get away for a while to try and remember what it was like to be just me again,' I continue.

'I reckon I feel the same way too from time to time.'

We sit together for a few moments more, munching biscuits and sipping our tea until it's time to get back to work.

'I'll be seeing to that washing now, Mrs B.,' Janet says and hands me her cup.

I get up to put the tea things away as she walks out of the kitchen. Then I follow her into the wash-house.

'My father spends a lot of time away from home,' Nabil tells me. We are sitting quietly together by the window eating nuts from the bag he brought me from home. 'He works very hard and has to travel a lot but I guess we're getting used to it,' the boy continues. He reaches for a pumpkin seed, opens it with his teeth and hands the pulp to me. It tastes salty and crisp. 'I mean, sometimes I actually feel glad he's not there.' Nabil pretends to laugh as he says this. 'He can be pretty strict with me sometimes, about my homework and things. Mum says it's because

I'm the only son.' He shrugs his shoulders and looks at me.

'I'll have another one of those pumpkin seeds, dear.' Nabil bends down to reach into the bag and I notice the back of his neck. It looks as soft and smooth as a child's. 'My father left us when I was very young,' I finally say.

'Left you?'

I nod. 'He went to South America, to Brazil. Said he had to find a way of making a living.'

'He came back to visit, though, didn't he?'

I shake my head. 'We never saw him again.'

He looks at me with wide-open eyes. 'Do you hate him?' Nabil asks.

'Sometimes I think that it must have been hard for him too, being alone in a foreign country and everything. At other times I wonder if he might have come back if one of us, Mathilde or myself, had been a boy.'

'Why would you think that?'

I shrug my shoulders. 'Sons are important to their fathers, aren't they?'

My grandson gets up, walks to the wastebasket and throws the pumpkin seed peel he has been holding in his hand into it. Then he walks back to the window. 'Shall we go out into the garden now, *Sittoo*?'

I am sitting on a blanket in the courtyard of our house. Mathilde is perched beside me and I am playing with a worn cloth doll. The doll's eyes are drawn on to a flat, fading pink face and her arms and legs are thin and gray with dust. I take off the doll's knitted dress and rub her body all over with my hand. Mother and Father are sitting on straw stools by the front door but I am only vaguely aware of their presence. Mathilde reaches out a dark, plump hand and grabs one of the doll's arms. I try to push her away and she swings back slightly, nearly toppling over. She lets out a scream and Mother turns her head sharply towards us.

'Salwa, is your sister all right?' Mother asks.

'She's not letting her play with the doll,' Father intervenes. 'Salwa, let Mathilde have the doll for a minute.'

I let go of the doll and Mathilde hugs it to her. I am angry because I have not yet finished giving the doll her bath. I make a face and stick out my tongue at my sister but she takes no notice. I turn my attention to my parents.

'It's a ridiculous name,' Mother is saying. 'No one in the village knows how to pronounce it and she'll be stuck with it for the rest of her life.'

'Mathilde is a beautiful French name; she'll appreciate it when she grows up.'

'And where is she going to grow up? She'll be staying here and no one will think so highly of the foreign name you've chosen for her.'

'You never know,' Father replies, suddenly standing up.

'What do you mean?'

'I mean maybe we'll go away one day, go and make lives for ourselves in a country where life is big, where there are better opportunities for everyone.'

I watch my father open the front door. He is halfway inside when my mother speaks up: 'We can't leave. This is our village, our home. Why would we ever want to go anywhere else?'

My father turns away from my mother and steps into the house. I snatch the doll back from Mathilde, pinch her hard and wait for her to cry.

The lights are on and although I am lying flat in the bed, I have no plans to fall asleep. I lift my hands in front of me and inspect them. They are misshapen, the fingers leaning sharply to one side, and no longer feel like hands should. I make a fist with one and marvel at the ascending line of swollen knuckles. My doctor son tells me there is nothing to be done about them, that I must accept the unsightliness along with the pain. I put them down and try to move my legs. I watch the shapes my feet make as they open and close under the covers but my legs will not budge. I look down sternly at them and will them to shift slightly, knobby knees and all, and then I laugh at myself out loud.

'Are you all right, Mrs B?' A nurse walks into the room. She comes up to the bed and looks down at me. I smile weakly but say nothing. 'Shall I turn the light off now so you can go to sleep?' She pats my shoulder and walks away, darkness in her wake.

'Dad says he's going to take part in the concert at the town hall next week,' May tells her sisters as they sit round the kitchen table having their breakfast.

'You mean the one they're having to raise funds for the troops?' asks Lilly.

May nods. 'But he won't tell me what he's going to do,' she continues. 'Do you know, Mum?'

'He hasn't told me anything about it,' I say. 'Eat up, girls. I want to tidy up the kitchen. I'm having the ladies over for coffee this morning.'

I suspect there are many things that Adnan and I don't tell each other but I am intrigued nonetheless. I ask him about it later that day as we sit together in the sleep-out.

'Just wait and see,' he says and smiles quietly to himself.

It is a fine night and almost everyone in the town comes to attend the concert. The girls and I are sitting near the front and May is already commanding the attention of many of the young men there. Mrs McCornick begins with a lovely piece on the piano and we all clap and cheer as the stage curtain opens and the performances begin.

Halfway through the concert Mr McCornick announces, 'Now let's all give a big hand to Mr B, who is going to perform a Middle Eastern sword dance.'

Someone in the audience titters as my husband walks on stage. A bright red sash is tied round his waist and he is carrying a large stick in one hand and a makeshift shield in the other. He stands perfectly still until we hear the sound of a gramophone play the music of back home. Suddenly, Adnan lifts the stick and shield above his head and takes a leap, landing lightly on one knee with the other leg bent before him. He shakes his shoulders up and down in time to the music. He taps his foot several times and shouts 'hey' in a voice I have not heard before. When he stands up again and begins to rotate the stick above his head, banging it against the shield every now and then for impact, the audience lets out a cheer and claps to the music.

'Mum, he's wonderful,' Diana whispers in my ear from her seat next to mine.

I nod and smile but I cannot take my eyes off my astonishing husband. The music rises and falls, and Adnan continues to move about the stage with light feet and happy heart, and as he takes his final leap, sword and shield held high, the people around us stand up, clapping loudly.

'You brought the house down,' I tell Adnan once we are back home.

He shifts round in his armchair and smiles. 'They enjoyed it, didn't they?' he says.

'I never knew you could dance like that, Dad,' Diana tells him when she walks into the living room to join us.

'There are lots of things you don't know about me, dear.'

Diana sits beside me on the sofa. I pull her close to me, look carefully at Adnan and see triumph in his eyes. 'Dad's full of surprises, isn't he?' I say, burying my face in my child's hair.

Nabil puts the straw in my mouth and tells me to sip the orange juice very slowly.

'Just a little bit at a time, *Sittoo*, so you won't choke on it.' He is a gentle boy, although I know there is a great deal of energy in him that he suppresses when he comes here.

'I've had enough now, dear, thank you,' I say a moment or two later.

He places the glass on the bedside table and picks up the soft drink bottle he put aside earlier. 'Are you all right, *Sittoo*?' Nabil asks between sips. 'Can I get you anything?'

'Why don't you get the photos you brought with you from the dresser, *habibi*? We haven't really had a good look at them yet, have we?'

He brings them over to me, helps me put on my reading glasses and sits next to me on the bed. He bends his head next to mine and I can smell the scent of his hair and hear him breathing. 'That's one of Daddy at his office. I took it of him just before I came here.' Riyad has grown older since I last saw him but he is still a handsome man and I feel a rush of tenderness come over me at his image. 'And this is of the whole family at the beach. The girls look quite grown-up now, don't they?' Nabil's two older sisters stare out of the photograph with huge grins on their faces. 'I do miss them,' he says quietly.

He lifts another photo from the pile and hands it to me. 'This is me and Dad up at his village in the mountains.' Nabil and his father are standing with a couple and a young girl in a garden with a large stone house behind them. Except for the woman, they are all looking at the camera and smiling.

'Whose house is it?'

'The mother's a cousin of Dad's. She lives in the house

with Yasmeena, that's her daughter.' Nabil points to the young girl.

'She's beautiful. Is she your age?'

Nabil shrugs his shoulders. 'I've only met her a couple of times. I think she's a year or so younger than me. She's not very happy. She told me her father only comes to visit them every once in a while because he lives in Beirut.'

'Poor young thing, without her daddy nearby,' I whisper.

We look at the rest of the pictures in silence until I lay my head back on the pillow and ask Nabil to help me remove my eyeglasses. 'Oh, dear. Oh, dear.'

'What's the matter, *Sittoo*? Are you all right?'

'I think I'll have a little rest now.'

I feel Mathilde leaning against me. 'Wake up, Salwa,' she says, breathing against my face. 'Wake up.'

I open my eyes to see my sister sitting up in bed. 'Go back to sleep, Mathilde, or Mama and Baba will hear you and get angry.'

'No, Salwa. Get up now. Let's go and look at the moon.'

I sigh, sit up and lift off the covers. 'What's the matter? Can't you sleep?'

Mathilde sniffs and shakes her head at the same time.

I fetch our slippers from underneath the mattress and once I've put mine on tell her to do the same. 'Shhh, do it quietly, Mathilde. Here, wrap this blanket over your nightie and I'll take Mama's shawl.'

We open the front door and shuffle into the courtyard. 'It's so dark,' Mathilde cries.

'You're six years old now,' I tell her impatiently. 'Much too old to be scared.'

I take her hand and walk to the edge of the courtyard. My sister shudders in the darkness beside me. 'Wrap the blanket tightly round you, Mathilde, or you'll catch cold.' It is very quiet and although I am also afraid I do not say so out loud. 'See how huge the sky is, Mathilde. Baba says it's as big as the whole world.'

She sighs and squeezes my hand. I lift up my head and hold my breath.

'Have we found it yet, Salwa?' Mathilde finally asks me. 'Have we found the moon?'

I put the photograph in the drawer beside my bed and instruct Lilly to take it out the next morning. She has been a little late in coming and I am anxious to tell her what I have found out. 'That's the house I was born in, dear,' I tell my daughter. 'It's back to the way it used to be. Isn't it wonderful?'

She adjusts her glasses on the bridge of her nose and looks closely at the photograph.

'That's not the place Aunt Mathilde was living in when we went to see her,' Lilly says, shaking her head.

'You're not looking at it carefully, dear. Look at those beautiful arches and the courtyard in front. Aren't those lovely flowers in the garden?'

Lilly shakes her head again. 'But what are Riyad and

Nabil doing there? And who are those other people with them?'

'Nabil said something about the house belonging to a relative of his father's, but the boy is wrong,' I say with a wave of my hand. 'I would know my own home, wouldn't I?'

Lilly takes off her glasses and returns the photo to the drawer. 'Of course you would, Mum,' she says quietly. 'You seem to be feeling a little agitated today. Shall I call the nurse to come and give you your bath now?'

I wait to see you again, Father, thinner than I have known you and older. I will call to you and watch for an instant as a stranger's look passes over your face before you finally run to hold me. Then, as clouds sweep invisibly over the moon above us and the air seems suddenly restless to move on, you will take my hand and walk me back to where we started from all those years ago, past the pain and bewilderment and all the living in between.

I am sitting at the window when Richard walks in. He places a chair beside me and sits down.

'Did he make it to the plane?' I ask.

'He got there in plenty of time but I stayed on until the plane took off.'

I nod and adjust the collar of my robe.

'He said to give you a big hug and kiss for him,' says Richard. He holds me close to him for a breath or two.

'Was he happy to be going back?' I ask, once my son has let me go.

'Yes, he was.'

I tap the window with my finger and point at nothing in particular. We sit quietly, looking out for a few moments.

'You look tired, Mum. Perhaps you should get into bed for a little rest before dinner,' Richard finally says. He lifts me into his arms and lays me gently on the bed. 'Goodness, you're as light as a bird,' he says, straightening up. 'We'll have to fatten you up a little.'

I close my eyes and open them again. Richard is almost out of the door. 'Tell your sister, dear . . .' I begin.

'Yes, Mum, what is it?' he asks, turning to look back at me.

'Tell her I just meant the house looked very familiar, that's all.'

Richard nods and lifts up his hand in a kind of salute. 'Sweet dreams, Mum.'